Weekly Reader Books presents

The Kids' Candidate

JONAH KALB
Illustrated by Sandy Kossin

HOUGHTON MIFFLIN COMPANY BOSTON

This book is a presentation of
Weekly Reader Books

Weekly Reader Books offers
book clubs for children from
preschool through junior high school.
All quality hardcover books are selected by
a distinguished Weekly Reader Selection Board.

For further information write to:
Weekly Reader Books
1250 Fairwood Ave.
Columbus, Ohio 43216

Library of Congress Cataloging in Publication Data

Kalb, Jonah.
  The kids' candidate.

  SUMMARY: A mistaken posting of age limitations sets
thirteen-year-old Barnaby off and running, politically, for the school
committee of his Massachusetts town.
  [1. Politics, Practical—Fiction. 2. School stories]   I. Kossin, Sandy.
II. Title.
PZ7.K12349Ki   [Fic]   75-17027
ISBN 0-395-21893-4

For Jan

1

Copley, Massachusetts, is almost thirteen miles due west of Cambridge and, as towns go, it takes its schools pretty seriously. There are ten of them — six elementary, three junior highs, and one high school. Almost nine thousand kids attend, roughly one out of every three persons living there.

Including thirteen-year-old, eighth-grader, Barnaby Brome.

"Yechchchchchchchch," said Barnaby to no one in particular. In room 212 in the new wing of Jennings Junior High, Miss Roberta Snell had just told her class that everyone would spend the morning taking the Cereban Aptitude Test. The test was known to teachers and students alike as "the CAT."

"Barnaby," Miss Snell asked, "did you say something?"

"Why do we have to take another CAT?" he asked belligerently. "We took one last year."

"Everyone in the school takes the test each January," she explained. "These tests are very, very important." Barnaby noticed that she didn't say why.

"Yechchchchchchch," he repeated, this time joined by at least six others. Actually, Barnaby's yechchchchchch probably spoke for twenty-five of the thirty kids in the class. There were one boy and four girls who didn't mind. They liked taking tests. They loved taking tests. "My father is a professor at Harvard," Julie Mitchell once explained.

It's kids like that, Barnaby thought, that make school . . . His thoughts trailed off, as they often did. Barnaby didn't think in complete sentences. He thought in flashes, and he wondered whether other people thought in flashes, or if he was special that way. Did Miss Snell think in full sentences, he wondered? He must remember to ask Billy.

Billy White sat next to Barnaby, and was Barnaby's best friend. Billy was one of the yechchchchchchers, too, even though his father was also a professor at Harvard.

"Everyone sharpen three pencils," Miss Snell intoned, and Barnaby and Billy leaped up to start a line at the pencil sharpener on the wall. Barnaby's pencils were sharp enough. So were Billy's. It was an excuse to get up and cause a little commotion.

Barnaby ground away at the pencil sharpener very, very slowly . . . mostly to annoy Lester Wagner and Julie Mitchell, and even Frank Feldman, all of whom were lined up behind Billy, who was behind Barnaby. And as he ground on, and on, and on, he remembered what had happened to him after the last CAT. What happened was, he threw up.

"Move," said Lester. Barnaby moved. He pushed back against Billy, and Billy pushed back against Lester, and Lester pushed back against Julie. Lester's pencils were pointing the wrong way, however, and they jabbed into Julie, who loved to take tests.

Serves her right, thought Barnaby, as she yelped. Barnaby relinquished his place at the sharpener, and his thoughts went back to the last CAT.

Barnaby had eaten four Oh Henry bars and two pieces of pizza that day before the test. It was the combination of those delights, rather than nervousness over the test, that had created the havoc. But the school didn't know that, and when he was being sick, his teacher had assured him that they would take "his condition" into account when grading. "We make allowances," he was told.

Barnaby wondered whether it was worth trying something like that again. He really didn't like to have his aptitudes measured all the time. Oh, he probably had some aptitudes, he thought. He was a pretty good baseball player, and a pretty good hockey player, and an excellent table-hockey player. He was pretty good at building things, too. Just the other week, he built a whirly spinner for his older sister Martha, using two one-foot squares of plywood locked together with a spike. Sandwiched between the plywood squares was a ball bearing device so that one square slid over the other without friction. His sister could stand on it and whirl around and around, trying to keep her balance. Whirly things that you buy in a store cost eight dollars, he remembered.

But a CAT? That was vocabulary, and math and spelling. Who needed aptitudes in that?

Still, he tried. For about an hour he tried.

"Miss Snell, may I leave the room?" he asked, as the hour was up.

Miss Snell practically ran to quiet him down. "Quiet, Barnaby," she hissed. "The others are working. Why do you want to leave the room?"

"The usual reason," he stage-whispered back.

"Everyone is getting a break in another half hour. Can't you wait?" she asked.

"Don't think so," Barnaby said, putting a distressed look on his face and slowly rubbing his belly. A memory flashed across Miss Snell's mind. It was so vivid that she forgot to whisper. "Yes, Barnaby, YES. GO," she cried.

Barnaby ran. But when he turned the corner in the hall, he slowed to a walk again, stopping several times to peer through the glass windows of other rooms. Sure enough, everybody was taking the CAT. He thought about whistling, but decided against it, and entered the boys' room.

"VOTE MCKINSTRY FOR SCHOOL COMMITTEE. WHY PAY MORE?" said the streamer plastered on the bathroom mirror.

Now who, Barnaby wondered, would put a bumper sticker on the mirror in the boys' bathroom of Jennings Junior High? Who in the school could vote, besides the teachers, and didn't they have their own bathrooms? And what is a school committee? Then, he used the facilities.

When he emerged from the cubicle, he had a lot of it figured out. Adults, he reasoned, must have used the school auditorium last night, and there must be a political campaign on.

Barnaby carefully climbed up on the sink and removed one of his three sharpened pencils. With great care, he slowly filled over the "PAY MORE" so that it could no longer be read, and printed the word "NOT" in its place. Then, he carefully filled over the name "MCKINSTRY," and wrote his own full name above it. He jumped down and stood back to admire his handiwork. The streamer now read: "VOTE BARNABY BROME FOR SCHOOL COMMITTEE. WHY NOT?"

Mischief done, he returned to his classroom and the CAT.

True to her word, Miss Snell gave the class a ten-minute break shortly thereafter, and a reasonable number of kids headed down the hall in a hurry.

"You really ought to do it, Barnaby," said Billy White as he emerged from the bathroom, still drying his hands.

"Do what?" asked Barnaby.

"Run for school committee."

Barnaby laughed.

"Yeah," said Frank Feldman. "Why dod't you rud?" Frank was the best first baseman in Copley Little League, but had less CAT aptitude than anyone in the class. What he did have, however, was a stuffed-up head. He always had a stuffed-up head. Barnaby could never remember him when he didn't have a stuffed-up head. "It's ad allergy," Frank once told him.

"I don't think you should deface school property," said Lester Wagner, coming out of the bathroom. He was a son of Harvard, too. "Did you really feel you had to write on Mr. McKinstry's campaign poster?"

"Lester, go 'way," replied Barnaby.

Lester wasn't through, though. "Mr. McKinstry is a candidate for the school committee, and whereas I do not agree with his basic

philosophies, I will defend his rights to communicate," Lester pronounced. "This is one of the finest school systems in the world," he went on, "and you go about . . . "

It was not Barnaby who pushed him. It was Frank. And it was not Barnaby who was kneeling down behind him. It was Billy. But when Lester fell over backwards, it was definitely Barnaby who laughed first. Lester wasn't hurt, except for his dignity.

"You fools," he cried from his position on the floor. But when Frank cocked his arm as if to hit him, Lester ran down the hallway.

"What are you doing after school?" Billy asked Barnaby.

"Nothing."

"Good. Let's stop down at the town hall," Billy suggested. "I wonder if a kid really *can* run for school committee."

"That's stupid, Billy," said Barnaby.

"Well, maybe," said Billy. "We can ask the town clerk, can't we? And besides," he went on, "it's on the way to the Pizza King."

2

Billy didn't ask right away. First, he read the law pinned up on the cork bulletin board. Then he asked.

"May we please have some nominating petitions for school committee?"

"Scram, kids. I'm busy," replied the town clerk without looking up.

"Sir . . . " Billy began again. "Sir. My friend here wants to run for school committee. May we have some petitions?"

"I said beat it," the town clerk replied, this time raising his head and peering over his glasses at Billy. "You can't run until you're twenty-one . . . or maybe eighteen."

"No sir," said Billy, in his most polite voice.

"The law leaves the age blank. I read it very carefully."

The town clerk rose from his chair, menacingly — then changed his mind and came around the desk to read the law on the bulletin board.

Just how it happened that there was no age requirement for school committee is a bit complicated.

First, the federal government lowered the voting age to eighteen. Then, Massachusetts lowered the voting age to eighteen. Then, a big debate took place about how old a *candidate* should have to be to run for state-wide office, like governor or something, and that's when the trouble started.

The lower house of the legislature wanted the age for candidates lowered to eighteen, too, but the upper house wanted it kept at twenty-one. They argued back and forth for a few weeks, and then, the upper house gave in. Eighteen became the law.

Meanwhile, the state's education committee was working on their own law about school committees, and they had to put in an age also.

But they wanted to wait and see how the other debate came out. So they wrote the law, and left the age requirement blank, meaning to put it in later.

The typist typed it with the age left blank, and eventually, the printer printed it with the age left blank. Then, everybody forgot about it.

When the education committee's bill was called up, the lower house passed it without reading it, the upper house passed it without reading it, and the governor signed it without reading it. The education bill became law — and the age was still left blank.

Billy and Barnaby looked over the nominating petitions in the pizza joint. A very upset town clerk, after making four telephone calls, eventually gave them the petitions, then went to the bulletin board and ripped down the copy of the law before anyone else could read it. "Now scram," he said once more, as Barnaby and Billy ran out of the town hall.

"See," said Billy, "you get fifty voters to sign their official, legal signatures and your name goes on the ballot. Think of it. Barnaby Brome. School committeeman."

Barnaby was getting a little frantic. "Billy, you're nuts. I don't even know what the school committee is! Why should I run?"

"Because we need a kid on the committee, that's why. You want to keep taking CATs all your life? The committee runs the whole school system. And who are the schools supposed to be for, anyway? Us kids, right?" It was an impressive argument, thought Barnaby.

"So why don't you run yourself?" Barnaby asked.

"I can't win," said Billy, making the ultimate politician's judgment.

Barnaby stared at him. He still couldn't believe what was happening. "Tell me, Billy," he said, "what makes you think *I* can win?"

Billy looked as if he were waiting for the question. "Well," he began, "you have an older sister. That means we can get the older kids to support you and we get the female vote at the same time." He paused for effect.

"Then, for another thing," he continued, "you're not stuck with the Harvard brand, the way I am. My father being a professor kills it for me. I can't be the common-kids' candidate, the way you can." Barnaby didn't react.

"Also, your name begins with a B, and you will probably be first on the ballot. You'd be surprised how many people vote for the first name on the ballot, no matter who it is." Barnaby was beginning to be impressed with Billy's political savvy.

"Then again," Billy went on, "your first name is Barnaby. Nobody would think that's a kid's name. It's just too old-fashioned."

"Now wait just a minute," Barnaby began. He resented that remark. But Billy just kept going.

"Last but not least," Billy concluded, "you're the only kid I know who would let me be his campaign manager. We're best friends, aren't we?"

"Kids don't vote," said Barnaby. He and Billy ordered a cheese and tomato pizza to split between them.

"Right," said Billy. "Kids don't vote. But their parents do. Every kid has a parent. Most have two. If we get the kids to campaign hard, just with their own parents, you can win."

They waited silently for the pizza, Barnaby desperately trying to think of a way out of it. The pizza came.

"Well," asked Billy, "will you do it?"

"Yaaaaaaaaah," said Barnaby, as he bit into his first pizza wedge. The pizza was very hot.

Billy leaped up and reached across the table to shake Barnaby's hand. "I knew you'd say yes. I just knew it. I officially accept your appointment as campaign manager. First meeting after school tomorrow, in my basement. We've got to get these petitions signed. Leave everything to me, Mr. Candidate. Just leave everything to me."

Barnaby was still fanning his mouth.

3

"We are gathered here today, friends," Billy began, "for one of the most important decisions of our lives." Billy was a Presbyterian and picked up his speaking style from his minister, Barnaby thought. On the other hand, Barnaby didn't know much about campaign managers. Maybe they all spoke that way.

Eleven kids, not counting Barnaby or Billy, were sitting around the semifinished basement of Billy White's house. It was a strange group. The oldest may have been sixteen, but most were nearer ten. Three of them were girls, including Martha, Barnaby's older sister. Barnaby wondered where they all came from. He didn't find out until later that there was one each from every school in Copley, and two from the high school.

To say that the kids were excited, or even interested, right away would be exaggerating. In truth, while Billy was explaining about elected school committees, Kathy Moo flipped the switch on Billy's old electric trains, and Jimmy Stephens began playing Ping-Pong with Eddie Ellis. When Billy began talking about how important the school committee was, Chris Bort began fooling with the ball in a broken pinball machine, flipping it with his finger.

"Come on, guys," implored Billy. "This is important."

"Yeah," said Frank Feldman. "Cub od."

Whoooooo, whoooo went the train whistle.

But then Billy told them how he and Barnaby had gone to the town hall, and read the law, and discovered that a kid could run. He told them about the town clerk, and the petitions, and soon everyone was paying attention.

"Who are the schools for, anyway?" he asked with passion. "For the teachers? For the voters? Or for us kids?" And then, he dropped the bombshell. "We need a kid on the committee. Let's elect one of our own. I say, let's run our own candidate. The kids' candidate. Let's run Barnaby Brome!"

Deathly silence in the basement. The only sound was the train, running around and around its track. And then, a giggle, becoming louder and louder, until it was a full-sized laugh. It was Martha.

"You can't run a kid. They won't let you," Chris Bort said.

"They can't stop us," replied Billy. "The law is the law."

"Kids can't vote," Kathy Moo said. "Who would vote for Barnaby?"

"Kids can't vote. That's right. But here's our plan," Billy replied. "Every kid has a parent. Most have two. We campaign strictly among the kids. Get every kid out, working for Barnaby. Then, each kid is given the job of convincing his own folks. That's all."

"I cad't codvidce by paredts to do adythig," sniffed Frank Feldman, sadly.

Whoooooo, whoooooo went the train whistle. Kathy Moo finally cut the power.

"You're going to campaign strictly among the kids?" asked Jimmy Stephens, unbelieving.

"Strictly among the kids," Barnaby said. He

figured it was time for him to say something. He was the candidate, after all. "We ignore the adults. Every kid has the job of convincing his own folks."

A long pause. Everybody was waiting. Then, at last, Chris Bort broke the silence. "Well. It's different."

Billy could have kissed him. Chris was one of the high-school kids, and if he went along, well . . .

Mrs. White came down the basement steps with cider and cookies, and the caucus broke up into small groups for argument and refreshment. And by the time the cider was gone, it was all decided. Barnaby was the candidate, and all eleven kids were ready to go. In their own ways, and for their own reasons, each and every one of them hated something at school. Each of them believed that change — almost any change — would be better.

"How do we start? What do we do now?" Christine Bridges asked.

Billy began passing out petitions. "Take a petition. Get your parents and some neighbors to sign . . . exactly as they are on the voters' rolls. Ring a doorbell and say you're collecting signatures for Barnaby Brome for school committee. People will sign. People sign anything. They won't ask you anything about the candidate. Get ten signatures on each petition. That way, we get over a hundred signatures, and fifty of them will be right. That's all we really need. Fifty."

"What do you do if someone asks about Barnaby?" Chris wanted to know.

"Don't say anything. Just take the petition to another house," Billy replied.

Billy stood at the head of the stairs, and shook hands with each of his campaign workers as they filed out of the basement with petitions in hand. There was some backslapping, and arm punching, and one more high giggle from Martha. But they had the petitions. That was what mattered.

4

At dinner that night, Martha looked terribly pleased with what she was eating, and considering that it was fish, Barnaby knew that she had talked. He drowned his own plate with ketchup.

"That's what the school cafeteria really needs. More ketchup," his mother said. "What do you think, Barnaby?" And she smiled.

"All right. So you know. Big deal. Pretty soon the whole town will have to know, anyway," Barnaby said.

"I happen to think it's a good idea, Barnaby," said his father, reaching for his wallet. "And here's your first campaign contribution. One dollar. Don't use it to bribe anyone, though." He chuckled.

Barnaby took the dollar.

"I mean it about the ketchup," his mother went on. "If I could have the ketchup contract — and maybe the french fries contract — we can all be rich."

"Ha ha," said Barnaby, sadly. He wished his parents would keep out of this.

Barnaby left the dinner table without his dessert and sat in the far corner of the living room, facing the TV set. He stared at the gray screen, trying to think. His mother thought it was a big joke, right? His father thought it was a big joke. His sister thought it was a big joke, though she didn't count much. But what did he, Barnaby, really think?

Well, first of all, he thought it was really Billy's idea, not his. And he wondered if the Harvard tag was Billy's real reason for not running himself. But then, thought Barnaby, there really was a lot of feeling about professors' kids. At least his own father was just an accountant.

He noted with pleasure that when the eleven kids met in Billy's basement nobody — not a single one of them — suggested any other candidate. It was as if it didn't matter who ran, just so long as it was a kid. Should that make him feel good? Or bad? His ideas were trailing off again.

He also had to admit it. He liked the idea. At least, he liked the idea of running. It would be fun. He was just a kid, like any other kid, he thought. Maybe different, but still, the same. Pretty average. And how often could a pretty average kid get to run for a public office? Maybe, he thought, if he could win school committee at thirteen, he might run for mayor at fifteen, governor at eighteen, and then . . . who knows . . . President, maybe, at twenty-one?

Then, he thought some more. Running would be fun. He was sure of that. But just suppose he won! Did he really want to be on the school committee? Meetings every Monday night. Reading. Ketchup contracts. Yechch-chchchch.

Which reminded him of the CAT. Just what were his real aptitudes? Maybe what he was really good at wasn't even taught in school. Maybe he really had an aptitude for politics. Maybe. Maybe. After all, he wrote on that streamer in the bathroom, didn't he? Maybe all this really was his idea, and not Billy's.

He knew one thing. If ever he was elected to the school committee, Miss Roberta Snell would be hearing from him. And he switched on the TV set.

"Good evening," said Walter Cronkite from inside the set. Barnaby quickly switched it off, and watched Cronkite collapse to a small white dot, and fade away.

The telephone rang, in the kitchen, and Barnaby could hear his mother answering it. "Yes, Dottie, I'm fine. How are you? . . . Of course it's my Barnaby. Do you know any other Barnaby Brome? . . . I have no idea. The boys must have looked it up, don't you think? They certainly wouldn't go to all this trouble if Barnaby couldn't run . . . Oh, I don't know. Maybe they like his smile. Put it this way, Dottie: do you know any boy his age *more* qualified to run . . . No, I don't agree with you. I don't think your Sandy *is* more qualified . . . Dottie — listen. I don't care what Sandy's scores were on the CAT. I still don't think he's more qualified than Barnaby

. . . Well. You may certainly vote for whomever you please . . . You do that, Dottie. You just do that." And she hung up.

"You're watching a blank screen?" Barnaby's father had wandered into the living room.

"I'm thinking," Barnaby replied.

"Well, that'll be a change," his father said, settling himself on another chair and flipping the TV set back on.

That was mean, thought Barnaby. He knew his father was only kidding. He knew his father really wished him well. But he also didn't like to be the butt of other people's jokes. How would he survive a campaign, he wondered, where the whole town would be laughing? All the adults, anyway.

"Dottie thinks her Sandy would make a better school committeeman than Barnaby. Imagine the nerve." Barnaby's mother was still fuming as she entered the living room. "Barnaby. If for no other reason than Sandy, whom I can't stand, I really hope you run and win."

But what about me, thought Barnaby? Do I hope to run and win?

5

Billy White may have been the youngest
political genius of all time, for he certainly was
a genius. His insights into adult ways of
thinking were profound.

The ten petitions were back with one hundred and fourteen signatures, and not a single
adult had asked a single kid who Barnaby
Brome was.

Thirteen signers had said, one way or another, that they knew Barnaby Brome well,
and that they would be proud to sign a petition
for such a fine man.

Three people thought they were signing to
support the Boy Scouts. The kid with the
petition was on his way to his weekly scout
meeting and was wearing his uniform.

A large number of people signed because they thought that any committee would be better than the one running the school system now.

Four people thought Barnaby was a professor at Harvard.

Billy's shrewdness, however, was beginning to show in other areas, too. Along with the eleven original school leaders, the meeting in his basement the following afternoon was joined by Lester Wagner.

"Why did you have to bring Lester?" Barnaby asked him. "He's a bag of wind."

"Exactly," said Billy. "This campaign needs a bag of wind. Lester opposed the whole idea when I first talked to him. He thought we were making a mockery of 'the best school system in the world.' But then, I offered him a job. Press secretary . . . You know, handling all the newspapers, and radio, and TV. Before he finished yakking about how bad the idea was, he accepted the job. Stand over there, Barnaby. Lester has to take your picture."

Lester pointed his father's Polaroid camera at the candidate.

"Cheese," said Barnaby, but he wasn't happy.

Billy checked the petitions once more, rolled them neatly, and called the meeting to order. Nobody paid any attention to him. "Come on. We've got to pick committees and go to work," he complained.

"You pick them," Chris Bort said. "I want to go to the town hall and watch the clerk when we hand in the papers."

"Let's parade," said Christine Bridges. She held up her baton and gave it a quick twirl.

Once more, Billy showed his political savvy. When kids want to parade, he thought, let them parade. We can pick committees later.

When the kids were on the street, Kathy Moo unveiled her first, and certainly her simplest, Barnaby Brome campaign poster. It said: "WHY NOT?" That's all that was on it.

And so, the parade, Eddie Ellis holding the poster aloft, moved down Elm Street, across Massachusetts Avenue, along Cedar Street to the town hall. Lester darted first to the right, then to the left, then in front of the kids, clicking away.

"Why not what?" asked a woman, wheeling a baby carriage.

"Why not Barnaby Brome for school committee," Billy answered. Christine flipped the baton in the air, and missed it coming down. Nobody seemed to care.

Inside the town hall, the paraders were well behaved. They lined up in two rows behind Billy, with Eddie holding the poster aloft.

"I can't take these petitions. You kids get out of here," the town clerk grumbled. The poster waved. The town clerk went on. "I'll tell you why not. Because you kids are just a bunch of troublemakers. I've a good mind to call the police, or your parents, or something. Now get out before I do it."

"Sir," said Billy, "the papers are legal, filled with legal signatures. You have to accept them."

"Kids, that's what you are." He spat it out, as if "kids" were the same as "criminals." "No-good, wild kids. I've a good mind to throw you out, by myself."

Eddie, taunting him, waved the poster once more.

The town clerk was menacing. "All right.

Give me those petitions. Now, you're trespassing on town property. I've got the petitions. Now scram, before you decide to run for town clerk."

Once more the poster waved "WHY NOT?" The town clerk, beside himself, threw the rolled-up petitions as hard as he could at the nearest parader . . . just as Lester's camera clicked.

6

The first week of the Barnaby Brome campaign was a week of contrasts. The adult world of Copley smiled, patted heads, patronized, snickered. But among the kids — furious activity.

The Copley *Sentinel* took Lester's announcement news release, with Barnaby's picture, and could hardly believe it. "Look at this," said the reporter, laughingly calling his editor over. "We got a thirteen-year-old kid running for school committee." The editor read the release, laughed, and was about to walk away when Lester insisted that he call the town clerk's office. He did. A grumbling, muttering town clerk confirmed that proper nomination papers were on file.

The *Sentinel* ran Lester's news release just as he had written it, without change, without comment, and without correcting the spelling errors.

Economy candidate McKinstry, who had first pasted his streamers in the boys' bathroom in Barnaby's school, and who, therefore, was indirectly responsible for Barnaby's candidacy, welcomed Barnaby into the race. But when interviewed by the *Sentinel*, he wondered out loud whether Barnaby could stay up late enough at night to attend all the meetings.

Professor Armand Collier, Harvard Ph.D., who had joined the race for school committee as a "serious" candidate, dismissed Barnaby out of hand. His statement to the press was that he thought educators, such as himself, should run school systems . . . "not money men, and not kids." He added that he thought Barnaby should at least get through junior high school before trying to run the whole school system.

Winifred Nobber, another "serious" candidate, told the *Sentinel* that, as a mother, she was interested in getting more education into the education system, and that she believed that Spanish, as well as French, should be started in the third grade "in order to keep this the best school system in the world." When asked about Barnaby Brome, she said she thought it was a practical joke, in poor taste, by a boy who probably didn't do too well on the Cereban Aptitude Test.

But among the kids, it was a week of discovery.

First, the central campaign committee — the original eleven and Lester — discovered that they were far better organized than the other candidates in the race, "probably because we're smarter than they are," Billy said.

Second, they discovered how much support they had in the schools. Not a single class president refused to join the president's council, working under the direction of the central campaign committee. Not a single member of that committee quit. Not a single fight broke out. Not a single kid missed a single meeting that was called. Nobody could remember so many kids voluntarily participating in anything with such good will and enthusiasm.

And the reason for this massive cooperation, and activity, was not hard to pinpoint. Barnaby was a kid — one of their own — a candidate like them. And, like Barnaby, almost every kid, in every class, in every school, really had something he hated about the schools, and hoped to express that to someone who would listen.

"Spanish in the third grade," cried Melissa Franklin. "That's RIDICULOUS!"

The biggest job of that first week, however, belonged to Chris Bort, the high-school student appointed head of the policy committee by Billy. His job was to sift through all the suggestions and complaints, and come up with a meaningful program for improvement that Barnaby could use as his campaign platform. But he was deluged with so many suggestions, such anger, such strong feeling, so many complaints, that he finally had to put his foot down. "Positive suggestions only," he announced. "We'll take care of complaints after Barnaby is elected."

Out of the week of negotiation and discussion, Chris finally put together a Barnaby Brome platform — a five-article program for the campaign. It read:

Article I. *All bathrooms in all schools are to*

remain unlocked at all times. Incredible as it may seem to the adult world, many of the school bathrooms were locked to prevent group meetings, and "other dirty things" from going on — a fact that no other candidate even knew.

Article II. *All schools must offer at least a few courses that kids really want to take.* "I mean," said a class president from the high school, "Russian literature is okay, I suppose, but I want to learn about motorcycles. I'll take one, if they offer the other, too."

Article III. *All cafeterias, in all schools, must offer at least some foods each day that most kids like to eat. Hamburgers, sloppy joes, and pizza qualify.* "I don't know where they find that stuff," a junior-high president said, "but if they expect us to study, we gotta eat. And I don't mean salad!"

Article IV. *No new teacher may be made a permanent teacher unless two thirds of all the kids from his classes vote for him.* "Teachers think they only have to satisfy the principals. What about us?" a grade-school student argued.

Article V. *No homework for elementary schools. No more than one hour a night for*

junior high. No more than absolutely necessary
for high school. And no homework in any school
in the spring when the weather gets nice.
"Education is okay," said a junior-high spokes-
man, "but we have to keep it in its proper
place. We've got important things to do."

The hammering down, and refinement, of the
platform was a major success. It was a platform that Barnaby thought he could run on,
one that Billy thought he could win with, and
one that Lester thought he could get "good
coverage" on.

The printing of the platform was assigned to
Jimmy Stephens, new head of the literature
committee, and the campaigners were about to
call it a week when Frank Feldman of the
parade committee stopped everybody in his
tracks.

"I thigk we ought to do a studt," said Frank
calmly. "We ought to show everybody what
kide of support we got, while we still got it."

"A studt?" Billy asked. He genuinely didn't
know what he was talking about.

"What's a studt?" asked Barnaby.

"Dod't bake fud of by allergies," said Frank
testily. "Studt. Ess tee you edd tee. We got a

billiod kids od our side right dow. But you dow kids. Sood, they could be back workig od their bodel airplades. If we plad to do sobethig, let's do it dow. Sobethig big."

"Okay, Frank," Billy said. "What stunt do you have in mind?"

"Well, I albost hate to suggest it, but the adults will love it. Let's get every kid out this Saturday with a big plastic bag, and have a "clead-up-for-Bardaby day." Everybody will see us. Everybody will dow we're serious. Saturday."

It was more than just a suggestion. It was a campaign stroke of brilliance, and Billy, and Barnaby, and even Lester knew it was a winner. Frank's allergies didn't prevent him from thinking.

So the central committee was called in and told to convene the class presidents. And the class presidents were told to tell the kids.

And that's when WBL–TV got into the picture. On Saturday.

1

"Clean-up-for-Barnaby" Saturday broke sunny and bright, and unseasonably warm, considering it was the dead of winter. Holding town elections in March was a particular handicap, Barnaby thought, because going door to door meant trudging through snow and slush. But not this Saturday. By 9:00 A.M., a crowd of kids had converged on the village green such as had not been seen in Copley since the call for Minutemen in 1775. Armed with green, and tan, and orange trash bags, the kids were divided by Frank Feldman into ten-kid working crews, and dispersed to every nook and cranny of Copley. Frank was organized. He had a map.

Each crew had a poster proclaiming

"CLEAN UP FOR BARNABY" in big, bold letters — the result of a massive two-day effort by the artists working with Kathy Moo. "It was worth it," said Kathy later, "because we can use the posters again. We're going to clean up *with* Barnaby on election day."

Frank's instructions to the crews were simple. "If it doesd't grow there, and if it isd't paided, pick it up." The kids were to bring their filled trash bags to the front lawn of the Hill School, right in the center of town, where Kevin Morgan would have a table soliciting contributions, and where a large sign would proclaim Barnaby's platform. Barnaby himself would be available to speak to anyone who would listen.

One crew was sent early to the parking lot of the A&P supermarket, where economy candidate McKinstry was passing out his own campaign literature. The operation began mildly enough. The ten kids patrolled the parking area, and when anyone dropped a McKinstry flyer on the ground, one of the kids would sweep it up into his trash bag. But a little later in the morning, there seemed to be a simpler way to do it. The crew chief, with his poster reading "CLEAN UP FOR BARNABY", merely walked beside Mr. McKinstry with his trash bag open. And soon, shoppers began recognizing the efficiency of this new idea. They stopped for a McKinstry flyer, and deposited it instantly into the Barnaby Brome trash bag, most often without even bothering to read it. It seemed the most natural process in the world. And at one point, a line formed to pick up McKinstry folders and throw them away. It was weird. Mr. McKinstry went home early, shaking his head.

By ten in the morning, when the first collection crews had finished, there was a small, but not unimpressive, pile of colorful trash bags deposited on the Hill School lawn. By eleven, it had grown to a large pile, and by noon, an independent judge would have agreed that it was at least a modest hill. But a problem was developing.

"Frankie. We looked everywhere. There is no more trash. The town is clean as a whistle," reported one crew chief.

Frankie knew that Copley was a pretty clean town even before he began, but he had anticipated the problem.

"Go to the dubp, dubby. That's where all the trash is."

"But . . . but . . . but"

"But dothig. Get that trash ad brig it here!" Frankie commanded.

After that, things went smoothly again. "Clean-up-for-Barnaby" crews were arriving regularly again, each with trash bags filled at the town dump. The bags were heaved up on the pile, and by one o'clock, the modest hill of trash had become a small mountain.

That's when the WBL–TV mobile news van arrived.

Lester was the first to see the television news truck, and he jumped out into the street to direct it beside the pile of trash. He peered through the windshield at a face he had seen a thousand times, thrust his hand into the cab of the van, and said:

"Mr. Garrett. I'm Lester Wagner, press secretary for the Barnaby Brome campaign. Welcome to Copley."

Richard F. Garrett, anchor man of the midday, the six o'clock, and the late news, climbed down from the cab and shook Lester's hand.

"What's going on here?" he asked. "We got a telephone tip."

"I'm afraid I made that call," said Lester modestly, and he told him about the campaign.

"You mean a thirteen-year-old kid is running for school committee in Copley? And he's running by organizing the kids?" Mr. Garrett repeated a lot. He especially repeated things he couldn't believe.

"Yep," said Lester.

"Joe," Mr. Garrett called out to his crew still in the van. "Get the cameras out. We got a crazy here." And the TV crew began unloading the cameras.

It would be nice to say that things proceeded in an orderly fashion after that, but it simply wasn't so. For one thing, the enormous pile of trash was beginning to attract a crowd of adults, and the crowd was beginning to tie up traffic around Hill School. And the presence of the WBL–TV news van didn't help traffic either. A large number of pedestrians decided that something was up, and they were milling around the lawn, and the school, and in the road until the police arrived.

"Move along, now. Move along," Officer Barr said, signaling the automobiles, and gently shoving people out of the way.

"You can't do that," Mr. Garrett told him. "You are interfering with the constitutional right of free assembly," he told the police officer, who just stared at him, open-mouthed. "These are free elections." It was clear that Mr. Garrett wanted to make a little news, as well as report it. He was hoping someone would arrest him. But the officer calmed him down, and cleared the street, and moved the vehicular traffic without further incident, and Mr. Garrett began concentrating once more on what was happening on the lawn.

The biggest confusion began with the arrival of Mrs. Winifred Nobber, the "Spanish-in-the-third-grade" candidate. Attracted by the big crowd, she concluded that the Hill School lawn would be a good place to pass out her own literature, and to convince people to keep Copley's schools "the best school system in the world."

But Frank Feldman didn't think that was fair. The crowd, after all, was Barnaby's crowd. "You'll have to go sobewhere else,

Bissus Dobber," he said politely. "This is a rally for our caddidate."

"Blow your nose, young man," Mrs. Nobber began. "I'm going to stand right here. This is school property, and I'm running for the school committee, and I'm not going to move one inch — I don't care who drew the crowd."

"Dot wud idch?," asked Frank.

"Not one inch," replied Mrs. Nobber.

"Okay. But I asked you to leave dicely," he said. "Over here, fellas," he called out to the most recently arrived pick-up crew.

It was almost artistic. The first row of trash bags placed in front of Mrs. Nobber was all tan. The second row, placed on top of the first, was all green. And the third row was all orange. The three layers of trash bags formed a wall up to Mrs. Nobber's waist, isolating her from the crowd.

"Dot wud idch?" asked Frank again. Mrs. Nobber was so furious she could not reply. She sputtered, and stuttered and, as a new row of tan trash bags was being placed on the wall, she finally blurted out, "You kids will pay for this!" With that threat, she surrendered, kicked the wall, and left the scene with as much dignity as she could muster. Mrs. Nobber moved through the laughing crowd muttering "kids out of control" and "rudeness" and "disgusting," but nobody paid any attention to her. The camera crews were zeroing in on Barnaby, and checking out the equipment.

Mr. Garrett walked in front of the cameras and adjusted the microphone hanging from around his neck. "Testing, one, two, three, four, testing. This is Richard F. Garrett speaking. Testing, one, two, three, four. Test your mike, kid. Say something," he told Barnaby.

"Testing one, two . . . " said Barnaby.

"That's enough, kid," Mr. Garrett told him, and then went back to his own mike. "This is Richard F. Garrett speaking. Testing, one, two . . . How are we doing, fellas? Aren't you ready yet? We haven't got all day," he told the crew. He placed himself in front of the mountain of trash.

"Roll it," said the cameraman. The film began to roll, and Mr. Garrett began to speak.

"This is Richard F. Garrett, and I am standing here, amid a mountain of trash, in historic Copley, Massachusetts — a mountain of trash collected as part of the ingenious political campaign for school committee of Barnaby Brome . . . Barnaby Brome is a unique candidate here . . . indeed, he would be a unique candidate anywhere, for he is only thirteen years old . . . Barnaby's campaign is *of* the school kids, *by* the school kids, and *for* the school kids . . . and the trash collected here is a demonstration, he says, of how the kids in the town support him . . . This was 'clean-up-for-Barnaby day' in Copley. The kids picked it up. The kids bagged it. And the kids piled it here. Lord only knows where they found so much trash in this lovely, and I thought clean, suburban town . . . "

He turned to Barnaby, and the camera followed.

"Barnaby Brome . . . why are you running for school committee?" he asked.

Barnaby turned his head to look into the camera, opened his mouth to reply, and froze.

"I said, Barnaby, why are you running for school committee?" Mr. Garrett repeated.

Barnaby tried to answer. He knew the answer, of course. It was such an obvious question that he had even rehearsed for it. But with the wheels of the camera turning, with

the red light on, with the eye of the lens gaping before him and staring down his throat, he opened his mouth and . . . and . . . nothing.

Nothing came out.

Nothing.

The camera ground on.

And on.

Nothing.

Finally, with a wry smile, "This is Richard F. Garrett reporting, in Copley, Massachusetts, for WBL news."

8

Everyone but Barnaby sat around the television set at the Brome house as Richard F. Garrett began the six o'clock news. He led off with the President's flight to Brazil, followed with a fire in Somerville, and then reported an arrest in Cambridge. Then, there was an ad for a deodorant. After the ad, a report from Washington, and an editorial on gun control, and then . . . then . . .

A wry smile appeared on Garrett's face as he reported "a note of community interest," as he called it. "I was in Copley, Massachusetts, this afternoon," he began. Garrett played the tape straight, just as the cameramen had recorded it — piles of trash, and the introduction, and . . . well . . . everything.

Barnaby was in his room with no interest at all in the television news. He was half lying, half sitting, on his bed, his left hand inside his baseball glove, his right hand slowly and lovingly shaping and forming and reshaping and reforming the pocket. His hand worked on a small spot especially hard because it was still moist from the neat's-foot oil he had put there.

For a moment, he relived one of his better catches during the summer before, when he had gone far, far to his left, scooped up a hard grounder that was sure to go through for a hit, and thrown straight as an arrow to the first baseman for an important out in an important game.

I am running for school committee, Mr. Garrett — Barnaby's inner voice kept repeating and repeating — because the kids of Copley need one of their own kind to represent them. That was what he had rehearsed a hundred times. That was what he was going to say when the camera turned on him, and he stared into the black hole of the lens, and . . .

He threw his glove hard against the wall of his room. He could hear, at the far end of the house, the murmuring of the television set, but he had no interest in what was going on. He got off the bed to retrieve his glove, and was working the pocket again when that inner voice began once more. I am running for school committee, Mr. Garrett . . .

"Dinner," announced his mother. "Martha . . . Barnaby. Dinner!"

Barnaby didn't want dinner, but he put his baseball glove carefully back into the closet, along with his other "summer" sports equipment, and headed for the dining room anyway. By the time spring comes around, he thought, I'll be playing baseball and maybe no one . . . And besides, the reason I am running for school committee, Mr. Garrett, is . . .

Mrs. Brome put mashed potatoes and beans on his plate, and Mr. Brome was silently carving a roast. He put a slice on each plate, unfolded his own napkin, and, keeping his eyes on his plate, silently began to eat. Nobody said anything. Not even "pass the gravy." People reached, just so that they wouldn't have to say anything.

"Couldn't you talk at all?" blurted out Mr. Brome when half the roast was gone. He simply couldn't contain himself any longer.

"Sam!" shouted Mrs. Brome, warning him.

If Barnaby could have crawled through his chair, into a hole in the floor, he would have gladly done so. He settled for an uncomfortable fidgit and another bite of roast.

Then, silence again. Somewhere between a forkful of potatos and a slug of beans, Martha looked as if she might say something, but she gazed around the table and thought better of it. That's why when the telephone rang, everybody jumped.

"Hello . . . " Barnaby's mother said into the mouthpiece. "Yes, Dottie, how are you? . . . No. No I didn't see the six o'clock news on WBL. Was there something on?" She made a face as she listened some more. "Really . . . well, I'm sorry I missed it. We always watch another channel . . . No. No, I don't know what your Sandy would have done . . . Maybe he would have, Dottie. I just don't know . . . Yes, Sandy is a smart boy . . . Yes, yes . . . " And she made another face as she listened again. "Goodbye, Dottie," she finally said, and hung up.

The reason I am running for school committee, Mr. Garrett — went that inner voice again.

The dessert was chocolate pudding, one of Barnaby's favorites, but he ate that as he ate the roast, without knowing, without caring, without smiling, and without saying anything. He, and his whole family, had returned to the silence of the meat and potatoes.

The phone rang once more and Mr. Brome sighed. It was going to be a long evening, he thought.

Barnaby stood up quickly, before his father could pick up the receiver. "Whoever it is," Barnaby half shouted, "tell them we cleaned up the town!"

"Aha," grunted his father. "You *can* talk. How about that." And he picked up the phone.

Barnaby left the room in a hurry, and headed once more for his own sanctuary at the other end of the house. He heard his father say something about "the six o'clock news" but he wasn't very interested. He knew where his mother and father stood. They were ashamed of him.

Strangely enough, though, he wasn't feeling so bad anymore. Maybe it was the supper, he thought. He almost always felt better after eating. But more important, he thought, we really did clean up the town. What difference did it make if he was scared of a television camera? Lots of kids would be, he mused.

He took his baseball glove down from the closet shelf again, not so much for the comfort it would give him, but because he wanted to try out a new pitching motion. It will be spring soon, he told himself. Time to get ready.

He worked on the motion for almost half an hour and then his sister poked her head in the door and announced: "Billy White, and Frank Feldman, and Lester Wagner are here to see you."

"Send them back here," he said. She disappeared to do his bidding.

The big three of the campaign operation trooped into Barnaby's room and found him practicing pick-off moves to first base, even though he didn't have a ball. They draped themselves where they could, Frank and Lester on the bed, Billy in the chair.

"Okay," began Barnaby, seizing the initiative. "I blew it. Now what?"

None of the kids said anything. They looked down at their feet, and around the room, and at each other, and then down at their feet again.

"Aw," said Frank finally, "I'd've dud the sabe thig."

"That's not what we decided," retorted Lester quickly. Barnaby perked up.

"Decided?" he asked.

"We had a meeting," Lester went on. "But we couldn't figure out who was going to tell you."

"Tell me what?" Barnaby asked.

Nobody answered. Each was waiting for someone else to break the bad news, but nobody would begin. Finally, Lester again . . .

"It won't work," Lester said. "The whole thing won't work. We can't win with you as a candidate, Barnaby. And we can't make Billy the candidate anymore because nominations are closed. I wanted Billy all along. Anyway, it won't work. The whole campaign just won't work. We decided to forget the whole idea and quit."

"Why?" asked Barnaby. He was stunned.

"WHY?" Lester repeated. "Don't you know? Are you kidding? Don't you know anything at all about politics? You blew it. I get Mr. Garrett and WBL here, and you open your mouth and . . . and . . . Well, you made the whole campaign go up in smoke. Pffffthththththth." His last word was something between a hiss of air and a spit.

"Couldn't you just say anything at all?" Billy asked, pathetically, hoping there was an answer, but knowing it was too late even if there was.

Barnaby went back to his baseball glove, molding the pocket again with his free hand. So that's the way it is, he thought. They don't want me. "All right," said Barnaby. He almost spit it out. "It's off. The whole thing is off. I didn't want to do it in the first place!"

The boys were surprised by the depth of Barnaby's feelings, and they looked away uncomfortably. In truth, Barnaby's feelings were hurt, and he was angry. What's the big deal, he thought? So the television people were here and I didn't say anything. So what? I'll bet half the kids in the school would have looked at the lens and done the same thing, he thought. And who was I supposed to be representing, anyway? Kids, right?

But if that's the way they want it, his thoughts ran on, okay. And besides, he told himself, Lester is a crumb. Frank is okay, but

Lester always was . . . But what about Billy? I'm supposed to be Billy's best friend. He certainly was mine . . . His thoughts were racing again, in flashes. They were incomplete thoughts, one fitting on top of another, like a crazy picture. He could see the lens again, and the trash, and he could hear Lester saying something, but he wasn't focused. Everything was filtered through the red of his anger.

" . . . the finest school system in the world," Lester was saying, "and we should have a candidate . . . "

"Cut it out," Frank said, sharply, and Lester shut up.

Barnaby sank back into his thoughts. Billy. What kind of way is that for Billy to act? Barnaby felt a pain in the stomach, as if someone punched him there. It faded, though. And they cleaned up the town, didn't they? And who cares about Garrett, anyway? And who wants Lester around, the bag of wind? But Billy. Billy. Best friend Billy.

" . . . meeting tomorrow afternoon," Billy was saying, "with all the kids involved, and we'll tell them then." Billy stood up and headed for the door, Lester hard on his heels, anxious to get out. Only Frank hung back a little, sorry to be going, wanting to say something to Barnaby, but not knowing quite what. Barnaby didn't even look up. He was busy molding the pocket of his glove. Then, even Frank left silently.

"Barnaby?"

"Whaaaaaaat?" Barnaby said to his sister Martha at the door.

"I don't think what you did was so bad. I bet I would have done the same thing . . . and I'm older than you are," Martha said.

"Yeah, but you weren't the candidate!" Barnaby retorted.

"That's true. I just wanted you to know."

"Go 'way," Barnaby told her. Barnaby actually liked his sister pretty much.

The more he thought about it, the worse he felt. Oh, not about the campaign. The campaign would have been fun, but he was kind of glad there was now no chance of him winning. But Billy . . . Billy, his best friend.

Barnaby felt that he had lost something important, and losing it hurt his feelings, and his hurt feelings made him angry. Friends, thought Barnaby, should be better than that.

9

The meeting was at Billy's house, in the unfinished basement playroom, as before, and everyone was there, including Barnaby.

At first, Barnaby couldn't make up his mind whether to go or not. He was still hurt and angry. If they didn't want him, he thought, well . . . he wouldn't even go to their meeting. But he was curious. He knew the campaign was off, because it couldn't be done without Lester and Billy and Frank. But, in truth, Barnaby still couldn't figure out why it had to be that way. He still didn't understand the big "crime" he had committed. Still, he thought, if it was his funeral, he ought to be there. So he went.

It looked like a funeral, all right, though Barnaby had never actually been to a real one. When Eddie Ellis, the recently appointed "organizations" leader, trooped in, he looked sick. His "snow shovelers for Barnaby" were all set up and waiting for the next snow storm. He reported seventeen kids with power snow blowers, and almost seventy-five with shovels, who had agreed to the plan. And he thought he could get even more. But now . . .

Kevin Morgan, who headed the finance committee, was even further down in the dumps. His table beside the trash pile had collected eighty dollars and thirty cents, a good start in any campaign, he thought. And now . . .

It wasn't even clear to Barnaby why a meeting was even called. All of the leaders apparently knew what had been decided before they came, he thought, judging from their faces. They were cool in their greetings to Barnaby — a casual "hi," and then a quick look away. He thought he saw tears in the eyes of Christine Bridges, but he wasn't sure. She may have had a cold, he thought.

Billy began with his Presbyterian minister's voice. "We are here for the sad occasion of calling off the political campaign for school committee," he said. "You all know what happened yesterday at the trash pile," he added, "and the effect that has on all of us. I have asked Lester, here, to prepare a news release that . . . "

"What effect?" asked Bob Cannon. His father was a lawyer, and when everyone was worried about Barnaby's age, Bob was given the job of "keeping him in the campaign at all costs." He was doing his job.

"You saw the six o'clock news, didn't you, Bob?" asked Billy.

"Yep."

"Then you know what happened. I don't have to tell you what that does to all of us."

"Yeah, you do," argued Chris Bort of the policy committee.

Barnaby perked up. Maybe, he thought, there were some others that didn't think it was such a big deal.

"Barnaby froze up there, in front of the TV cameras," Lester chimed in. "I got the TV people here, and he froze up. Right now, we're the laughingstock of the whole town. And if we keep going, we're going to make a laughing-stock of the finest school system in the whole world."

"We had a meeting," Billy went on. "Lester and Frank and me, and then Barnaby. We agreed to call the whole thing off," he said with finality.

"Barnaby," Chris Bort asked from the back, "do you want to call the whole thing off?"

Barnaby was confused now. He thought everybody had decided. "Well," said Barnaby, "that's what I thought everybody wanted to do."

Frank Feldman thought it was time he said something. "You dow . . . be ad Billy ad Lester agreed, I suppose, but to tell you the truth, I dod't dow why I agreed. Like I told Bardaby, if I were stadding there, I would have dud the sabe thig!"

Frank's remarks started a hubbub among the other leaders. "It would have happened to me, too," said Mark Rider.

"We're not running this campaign for the TV people, are we? He's the common-kids' candidate, and he acted like a common kid. So what?" said Melissa Franklin.

"What about our program," Christine

Bridges cried out. "I mean, the open bathrooms, and the decent food in the lunchroom. That's why I'm in it."

"Order, order," cried Billy. Things were getting out of hand.

"Look," said Billy. "I know how you all feel. I feel that way myself. But you can't run a campaign without a candidate. Maybe kids aren't really ready for politics. They just aren't mature enough. My father said the TV show proved that . . . "

"Your FATHER!" cried Eddie Ellis.

Billy hadn't meant to let that slip out. But he was caught now, and the room quieted down, waiting. He went on: "Yes, my father. He was kind of 'for' this whole campaign idea when it started. But now, well, he says that if we go on with it, we'll make a laughingstock of the whole town, and the schools too. And if we ruin the reputation of the schools, he said, maybe I won't be able to get into Harvard when I graduate." Billy trailed off in his speech. He sensed that things weren't going right, but he didn't know how to correct them. "And you won't either!" he shouted at Chris Bort.

Billy scanned the faces in the basement, looking for support. He found none. He couldn't understand what happened. It was all arranged, he thought. He, and Lester, and Frank had agreed. And his father had said that . . . He sat down, confused.

So that was it, Barnaby thought to himself. Best friend Billy. Harvard.

Frank Feldman took over control of the meeting. "All right," he announced, "wud at a tibe. What do you all thigk?" He pointed to Chris Bort.

"I think the campaign to run a kid made sense before, and it makes sense now. Barnaby didn't commit any crime. He got scared. I'm for going on."

"I think," began Christine, "that all the scared kids in this town need someone to represent them on the school committee. I'm for going on."

"I think," said Eddie Ellis, "that we already know what the 'fathers' want. They run the school committee now. It's what the kids want that is important. I'm for going on."

"I think," said Jimmy Stephens, "that the bathrooms are still closed, that the food is still lousy, and that the teachers still don't teach what I want to learn. I'm for going on, too."

"I think," added Kathy Moo, "that we have not yet begun to fight."

"I'm for going on," said Melissa Franklin. "Me, too," said Mark Rider. Frank called on Barnaby.

"Well," Barnaby began, "I'll go on, of course, if you all want me. I'm sorry about what happened in front of the trash yesterday, but — you know — it's a very scary thing, that red light and that lens looking at you. But I have to admit, I don't think what happened was so terrible, either."

The tension that had filled the basement ever since the meeting convened just melted. Everyone was smiling again. Everyone, except . . .

Lester stood up, peered around the room, and made his own pronouncement. "Whether the campaign is off or on makes no difference to me. I resign. I just won't stand for the finest school system . . . " Everyone laughed. Lester climbed the stairs of the basement, and left.

The laughter stopped, and everyone turned to Billy.

"I guess I've resigned, too," announced Billy. "My father doesn't want me involved anymore. But I can't just up and walk out because it's my house."

Martha Brome rose. "Next meeting of the campaign committee leaders — those that are still in — is at our house . . . mine and Barnaby's . . . tomorrow after school. We'll select a new campaign manager."

To give Billy his due, he looked miserable.

"You dow what," said Frank Feldman. "I've got adother idea for a studt!"

10

"MAKE A DEAL WITH YOUR PARENTS
TRADE A VOTE FOR BARNABY
FOR TWO HOURS OF CHORES
WITHOUT COMPLAINING"

Jimmy Stephens, hockey player and head of the publications campaign committee, had been busy. "Just write it on the blackboard before the teacher comes in," he told all the class presidents. "We'll change the message every week. And if a teacher erases it, why just put it back up the next day."

And so it was that every classroom in every school in Copley displayed Jimmy Stephens' "make a deal . . . " slogan on the Monday morning after the trash weekend.

Not that it was easy to get everyone to agree.

"Kids in my class can't read yet," announced one class president. "Read it to them," replied Jimmy. "Show them the letters, one by one. Show them each word. Get the teacher to use the slogan in her reading lesson. Use your imagination," he implored.

"Why two hours?" another class president wanted to know. "That's a lot."

"Look," Jimmy said. "We're serious about Barnaby. If we don't give something important, how will your parents know how you really feel?"

"Okay," he said. "Two hours. Yechchchchchch."

Barnaby arrived at his homeroom class a little bit after most of the other kids, and immediately had to defend himself. He had to defend himself against rolled-up paper balls being thrown at his head, one or two erasers, catcalls, and boos.

"Two hours without complaining," cried a classmate. "Now you've gone too far."

But the kids were smiling as they bombarded him, and Barnaby knew that the attack was

really a way of telling him that everything was okay. He picked up what he could, and hurled it back blindly into the mass of his friends.

"Blame Jimmy Stephens," Barnaby cried from under the hail of missiles. "It was his idea." Another round of paper pellets hit him.

Barnaby peeked out from under his arms. Billy White was sitting quietly in his seat, doing nothing. Lester Wagner was reading a book . . . or at least pretending to be reading a book.

Miss Snell walked in. "All right, class," she commanded. "That will be enough! Quiet down this instant." She walked to her desk, opened her briefcase, and removed some papers without having even glanced at the message on the board.

"Anderson," she called out, beginning the roll call. "Appelbaum . . . "

The noise level in the classroom once more rose to a small din. Kids knew when their names would be called, having been through this exercise every day since the beginning of school. There was no need, or desire, to listen carefully to the calling of the roll.

"Brome," she said.

"Ouch," said Barnaby. The barrage had begun again, quietly, secretly, until Barnaby was hit by a pencil. His "ouch" coincided exactly with his name in the roll call.

Miss Snell looked up at the innocent faces before her, spotted Barnaby, and smiled. She decided that she would make her pitch right then and there, and she moved around to the front of her desk.

"Now, that's no way for a candidate for the school committee to behave, is it?" she inquired sarcastically. "A position on the school committee is one of very high responsibility, Barnaby. Do you really think you belong there?" she asked.

Barnaby said nothing.

"You know, I greatly admire the spirit of your campaign," she continued. "I really do. And the picking up of all the trash was very clever. Very clever politics, indeed. But running a school system is a complicated matter. You deal with teachers' salaries, and big budgets, and policy judgments, and matters surrounding the Cereban Aptitude Test, and . . .

It is especially complicated here in Copley, which, as you know, has one of the finest school systems in the world . . . "

Barnaby still didn't say anything. He correctly judged that she wanted to make a speech.

"In Copley, the school committee is called upon to direct the efforts of the entire system — nine principals, almost five hundred teachers and administrators. The budget last year was eleven million dollars, Barnaby. Do you know how much is eleven million?"

Barnaby said nothing.

"The school committee reviews the curriculum, Barnaby. Do you know what the word curriculum means, Barnaby?" She smiled.

Miss Snell thought she was making points. She thought Barnaby was paying careful attention to her words of wisdom. But she was wrong. Barnaby was reminding himself that teachers can make kids look dumber, and feel worse, than any other adult in the world, with the possible exception of parents. And teachers do it on purpose, he told himself, just to feel superior, and smarter than the kids they teach. They embarrass a kid in front of his friends.

For no other reason than that, he thought, the school committee needs a kid.

Barnaby hoped that Miss Snell was through preaching, but he wasn't going to get away that easily. He gritted his teeth, blanked his face, and would have gone on with the listing of the sins of teachers when both he, and Miss Snell, were interrupted by the rhythmic tapping of a pencil.

Dah dih dah, went the pencil, somewhere in the back of the room.

Miss Snell ignored it. "I think the whole campaign is very clever. It was very bright of you to find that you could run. But after the joke is over, I think you have to give serious consideration to the . . . "

Dah dih dah. Dah dih dah.

" . . . consequences of your action. The test of whether you belong on something like the school committee . . . " Dah dih dah. Dah dih dah. The tapping became louder, joined as it was by several other students. Barnaby switched off even his half-hearted listening to Miss Snell to see if he could discover what the pencil tapping was all about. He looked to the back of the room and saw two students, pencils poised for tapping, mouthing his name in cadence with the taps.

"Bar-na-by," they mouthed, as the pencils went dah dih dah. Other kids began picking it up. A good one third of the class was now tapping, in rhythm, dah dih dah, and smiling, and giggling, and mouthing his name. Barnaby smiled back at them, turned back around, and observed Miss Snell.

Miss Snell was distracted, but determined. "As I was saying," she continued, her voice slightly louder, her look slightly more harassed, "the test of whether you belong on something like the school committee is the degree of your maturity . . . " dah dih dah "your ability to see all sides of every action . . . " dah dih dah "your understanding of the implications of every decision . . . " dah dih dah "your understanding that schools . . . " dah dih dah " . . . are not . . . " dah dih dah " . . . just for the children." DAH DIH DAH, DAH DIH DAH, DAH DIH DAH.

The kids had abandoned the relatively mild pencil tapping. They were now slapping their palms against their desks in that special rhythm, louder and louder and louder, each of them mouthing the name "Bar-na-by." Miss Snell was more than flustered. She panicked.

"Stop that this instant," she yelled.

Everybody stopped.

Miss Snell took almost half a minute to collect herself. She then, very deliberately, walked to the corner of the room, took an eraser from the blackboard ledge, and removed Jimmy Stephens' campaign slogan from the blackboard with quick strokes. She then went back over the area, more carefully this time, being absolutely certain that no part of what he wrote could still be seen. Nose in the air, she returned to her desk, shaking. "Cooper . . . " she called out, continuing the roll call. "Crim-mons . . . "

The homeroom period ended with the bell, Miss Snell sitting at her desk already exhausted, and her teaching day had not yet begun. But nobody paid any attention to her.

"She had no right to make a political speech," one of the kids remarked as he passed Barnaby. "Yeah," said another. "If she can't stand the heat, she should get out of the kitchen. That's what my father always says."

Barnaby filed out with the rest, but Billy

White caught him in the hall just beyond the door. "Barnaby," Billy began. "Wanna go to the Pizza King after school today?"

Barnaby stopped and looked at Billy.

"No thanks, Billy," he replied. "Campaign meeting this afternoon," he said, and headed down the hall to his next class.

Best friend. Huh!

11

News of the incident in Miss Snell's homeroom class swept through Jennings Junior
High by the second period of the day, and by
some miraculous process known only to the
kids, the news skipped across town to Hill
School, and all the others, before noon.

Kids in all schools greeted each other in the
hallways with "dah dih dah," instead of the
usual "hi." In the lunchroom at Monroe School,
where the menu consisted of tuna casserole and
garden salad, the rhythm of "Bar-na-by"
clanged through the school building as the kids
pounded their silver on the lunchroom tables.

"It sounds like a James Cagney movie," one
of the teachers commented, "where the prison-
ers in jail are pounding on the tables."

"I suppose the kids sometimes feel like that," another teacher remarked. "As if they're in jail, I mean."

But tuna casserole or not, the students of Copley were happy. And it was Barnaby himself who first said why. "I think the kids feel they won something in the battle with the adults."

Dr. Richard Loomis, the remedial reading teacher in the high school, explained the same thing in bigger words to one of his colleagues, as he wrote out a ten-dollar check to the "Barnaby Brome Campaign Committee." "The kids are organized, at last," he said. "Using the Barnaby campaign, they feel they can express themselves through him. They feel powerful. They feel free. They feel that they are controlling events, instead of having events control them. It's really rather wonderful, when you think about it." Few of the other teachers agreed with him. They thought the kids were just out of control. But Dr. Loomis didn't mind. "If the teachers agreed with me," he speculated, "then it wouldn't be much of a victory, would it?"

"Dah dih dah," said Frank Feldman, as he

entered Barnaby's house for the afternoon meeting.

"Dah dih dah," said Martha, as she showed him into the living room.

When all the campaign managers had assembled, each committee reported, briefly.

Three hundred and fourteen bags of trash to the dump, minus the fifty they picked up *at* the dump. Not bad.

One hundred and seventeen dollars in the campaign bank account. Also not bad.

Eddie Ellis reported that "snow shovelers for Barnaby" now totaled ninety-seven kids with shovels, twenty-two with snow blowers. But no snow.

Melissa Franklin reported posters for Barnaby in every ice-cream parlor and every pizza joint in town except Frank's Pizza on Main Street. Mr. Frank told her that pizza and politics don't mix. Guido's Pizza Parlor, however, renamed his "special deluxe with everything" pizza the "Barnaby Brome special." Barnaby said he hoped Guido would leave out the anchovies.

In quick order, the executive committee of the campaign reassigned Mark Rider to be press secretary, replacing Lester, and appointed Frank Feldman as campaign manager. They voted a kid boycott of Frank's Pizza joint, over the objections of Eddie Ellis, who thought Frank's burger pizzas were the best in town. "You got to give up sobethig, Eddie," Frank Feldman told him.

"What's the new stunt, Frank?" Barnaby finally asked.

Frank tried to clear his head before making what he knew would be a long speech. He blew his nose, and went "hurrrrmmmpt" loudly, several times. But everyone knew it wouldn't work. Finally, he began.

"Before I tell you about the dew studt, let's figure out why the trash idea was so good." Barnaby thought Frank was getting a bit preachy but he admired the way he was trying to avoid nasal sounds.

"Trash Saturday was a success," Frank went on, "because all the kids were id it. Everybody. Every kid we dow participated. Right?"

"Right."

"Furthermore," Frank continued, "every kid did sobethig that he really hated to do. Like collect trash. But they did it adyway, because they cared. Right?"

"Right."

"You see," Frank said, "that's why it was such a success. Disciplid! Dobody liked it, but they did it — because they cared for Bardaby. They did sobethig that they wouldd't dorbally do id a billiod years."

"Is that million years, Frank, or billion years?" asked Eddie Ellis.

"Billiod," he replied, "with a capital ebb. Ad furtherbore, everybody could see what we did. It was very visible. Everybody could see that the kids really cared about Bardaby."

"Right," said Melissa.

"Come on, Frank. What's the new stunt?" Barnaby pleaded.

"Take it easy. I'll get there," Frank continued. "So those are the three thigs we need in a new stunt. Discipline. Every kid must be involved. Everybody in town must see it. Now it would also be super," Frank added, "if the stunt had something to do with the campaign."

The interest in the room was rising dramatically, but not because of what Frank was saying. For some reason nobody could understand, Frank's head was clearing up. The nasal sounds were coming out nasal.

"Frank . . . " began Eddie Ellis, in wonder, " . . . your nose . . . "

"Don't interrupt," Frank said, and then continued his speech. " . . . which brings me to what happened last Saturday with Barnaby and the TV cameras." He paused. Barnaby shrank in his seat. Martha squirmed. Everyone else turned aside. It was painful to even think about it.

But Frank plowed on. "Barnaby froze before the cameras. But you know something? I would have, too. And so would most kids. Barnaby didn't commit a crime. He just got scared, like me and you. He was silent because he's a kid. But we never told anybody that he wasn't a kid, did we?"

Silence.

"So here's the stunt," Frank said, at last. "I think that this Saturday, *every* kid should be silent!"

"Silent?" asked Eddie.

"Silent," wondered Christine.

"Silent like Barnaby?" queried Martha.

"Silent for Barnaby?" asked Kathy Moo.

"All day Saturday?" Mark asked.

"Silent," said Frank with finality. "Look at what it has going for it. It takes discipline. Every kid can participate. Every adult would know we're doing it. And it tells people that all the kids are really just like Barnaby, and that he's just like us. We're behind him."

There then followed the noisiest discussion of silence ever held. Kathy Moo thought that her artists could come up with a couple of thousand "Silent for Barnaby" lapel cards before Saturday with no trouble. Martha wanted to know why it had to be Saturday. "Wouldn't it be better if we could do it on a school day?" she asked. Kevin thought it would be a gas. Jimmy Stephens wanted more details.

"Do you mean no talking to adults, or no talking, period?" he asked.

"No talking, period," Frank answered. "Unless we did that, nobody would even notice. Half of us don't talk to adults now," he pointed out.

"What about talking to your mother and father?" asked Melissa.

"Especially no talking to your mother and father. That's who we are trying to impress with our discipline," Frank responded.

"I don't think my sister could do it," Jimmy said.

"Sure she can," Frank encouraged him, "if she wants Barnaby to win badly enough."

"I think that's asking an awful lot of kids," Eddie suggested. "It's really hard to keep quiet all day. I remember one day when I had to because they changed my braces. It was tough."

Even Barnaby complained. "You're taking something I'm ashamed of, and making it . . ."

But Kevin jumped in before he could finish, and before Frank could answer. "It's okay, Barnaby. Every kid understands how you felt. I think Frank is right. Silent Saturday."

The executive committee voted eleven to nothing for "silent Saturday," but without the joy that such a vote implies. All of them knew how hard it would be. Class presidents were to be convened the next day and told about it. And Kathy Moo was to get those artists working immediately.

"Dah dih dah," said Christine, as she left the house.

"Dah dih dah," replied Martha at the door, sadly.

"Frank," asked Barnaby, "forgive me for asking, but what happened to your stuffed nose?"

"I dod't dow," replied Frank.

12

Silent Saturday

Nine-year-old Roy Bates, running in his yard, tripped over a creeping vine on his mother's rose bush. He fell, face down, on the edge of a piece of slate, cutting his chin. When he put his hand up to his face, he saw the blood.

Tears welled in his eyes as he picked himself up and ran into his house. But his crying sounds were muffled by his will.

"What happened?" demanded his mother. "Oh, my poor baby," she cried.

No answer.

"What happened?" she demanded more insistently, looking at the wound and beginning to panic.

Roy turned and fled to his room. He found his "Silent for Barnaby" badge, put it on, and returned to the kitchen, tears streaming down his face, but making no sound.

He took off his coat as his mother cleaned his chin. He closed his eyes with pain, and squinted hard to distract himself.

It was really a minor cut. After his mother cleaned away the blood, she gave him a wash-cloth with ice, and then put a Band-Aid on it. After a while, sitting before the television set, even the tears went away.

Mr. and Mrs. Bates talked about it later. They decided that maybe they would vote for Barnaby . . . out of respect for their son Roy.

Laura Pearson and Alan Doherty went into Rickles Ice Cream Store and seated themselves at the counter. Laura and Alan had been in the high-school play together, and knew each other, and were sort of friends, but were not "going together" or anything.

Alan was nice, Laura thought, but he was so shy!

Ginny Lucia, who was wearing a "Silent for Barnaby" card around her neck, and who had also been in the high-school play, waited on them.

They waved a greeting. Then Laura motioned twice, as if she were scooping ice cream from a tub. She then imitated the motion of squirting chocolate syrup over the ice cream, shook an imaginary canister of whipped cream, and gently placed an imaginary cherry on top of the imaginary sundae she had just fixed for herself. Ginny understood perfectly.

Alan put his hand on an imaginary glass, and sucked up with an imaginary straw. Everybody smiled.

When they had finished their sundae and soda, Ginny made out two separate checks. To Laura's great surprise, Alan reached over and took hers, too. He paid for both. Ginny raised an eyebrow.

On the way out, Laura put her arm through his.

Silent Saturday was Marie Rolo's tenth birthday.

"Happy birthday," Marie's mother said when she woke her up. Marie opened her eyes and gave her mother a radiant smile, and a kiss.

She then leaned over to her night table and pinned her "Silent for Barnaby" badge on her pajamas.

Mr. Rolo watched with adult amusement as Marie opened presents from her brother, two sisters, Aunt Bess, and, of course, from his wife and himself.

Marie got a beautiful charm bracelet which she had admired in a store, two games, a book, two records, a new sweater, and ten dollars in cash. As she opened each package, her eyes lit up, and she rushed to the giver with a warm hug and a kiss. Even her brother kissed her back.

"You know," mused her mother, "it's really unfair, on her birthday, don't you think?"

"Life is unfair," said Mr. Rolo, but his admiration for his children was growing by the minute. He, too, secretly decided to vote for Barnaby.

Jimmy Macmillan had a problem. He was a paper boy, and Saturday morning was collection day. And yet . . . and yet, Jimmy was one of the very first "paper boys for Barnaby." He knew he could not be disloyal to the candidate he believed in. That would be like being disloyal to himself, he thought.

Jimmy's problem was, the seventeenth house on his route belonged to Mrs. Winifred Nobber, the "Spanish-in-the-third-grade" candidate. Oh well, he decided, maybe things will be okay.

He arrived at Mrs. Nobber's driveway, parked his bicycle, took a folded copy of the Boston *Globe*, together with the week's invoice, and rang the bell.

"Yes," said Mrs. Nobber, opening the door and peering at him as if she didn't know who he was. Jimmy pointed to the invoice on top of the paper.

Mrs. Nobber smiled. "I'm sorry, young man, but I seem to have left my glasses inside. How much do I owe you?" she asked sweetly.

No answer from Jimmy.

"Look here, young man," Mrs. Nobber continued, her voice a little rougher, "you'll just have to tell me how much I owe you. I can't read the bill," she said.

From out of Jimmy's back pocket came his tag saying "Silent for Barnaby." He carefully clipped it on to his jacket pocket.

Mrs. Nobber saw red. "How *dare* you, you impudent little . . . " She couldn't seem to find the right word. Jimmy was glad to see that she could read the tag without her glasses, all right. "I'm going to call your office this minute! I'm going to see to it that you lose your job," she said furiously.

Jimmy's hand went up in the traditional sign for "stop."

Mrs. Nobber stopped, smiled, came back to the door, certain as she was of victory. "Well, how much do I owe you?"

Jimmy reached in, grabbed the still folded copy of the paper from her hands, and ran for his bicycle.

"Why, I n-e-v-e-r . . . " he heard her sputter, but Jimmy didn't bother turning back. He was almost to the street when he heard the door slamming behind him.

Mr. Lawrence Rainey, district manager for New England Telephone, first noticed that something was wrong about noontime. "Hey," he said to his chief engineer, "what's wrong with the computer? There should be about seven thousand calls in Copley by now, and the computer shows only twenty-three."

The chief engineer looked at the dial and confirmed that there were only twenty-three calls in the whole town of Copley for the whole Saturday morning. He went around to the back of the machine to check that the plug was in. Then he put a test program into the computer and watched the meters.

"Everything checks out perfectly," said the chief engineer, scratching his head. "Is it possible," he asked Mr. Rainey, "that nobody in Copley is using the telephone this morning?"

"Nah. Not possible," said Mr. Rainey. "Copley is full of kids."

Lester Wagner called Billy White just before lunch.

"Hi, Billy. Whatcha doing?"

"Nothing," said Billy.

"Yeah. Me neither."

Long pause. Then, Lester again.

"What do you think of 'silent Saturday?' I think it's a stupid idea."

"Yeah," said Billy.

"You wouldn't have done that, would you, Billy? I mean, if you were still campaign manager . . . "

"I don't know," Billy said sadly. "I'm not the campaign manager anymore."

"Yeah," said Lester.

Long pause.

Long, long pause.

"Well, see you Billy," Lester said.

"Yeah," said Billy.

They hung up.

13

Barnaby couldn't quite hear the conversation in the living room, but, he told himself, he didn't really care that much. His father had told him that Professor Collier, Mr. McKinstry, and Mrs. Nobber had asked for a meeting with the adult Bromes, and that he had invited them over for tea. "It's really very flattering," Mr. Brome said. "Three important people like that, wanting to come and talk to us."

Barnaby wasn't impressed. If they wanted to meet with his parents, that was fine with him, but he thought that if they had anything to say as candidates, they should have been talking with him. After all, it was he, Barnaby, who was in the fight. His father and mother weren't even encouraging, ever since he froze in front of the TV camera on "trash Saturday."

That had been four weeks ago, thought Barnaby — and his campaign had been swinging along pretty well since then. Silent Saturday, from all reports, had been a great success. And then, there was that incident at the League of Voters' Candidates' Night, at the high-school auditorium.

The league always invited the candidates on a well-advertised special night to speak to whomever showed up, and discuss the issues. Not too many people come to that kind of meeting normally, but even so, Barnaby and his executive committee were really angry that Barnaby wasn't even invited. Frank called the league president, and she told him that the league was only inviting candidates "old enough to vote themselves," she said. "We are, after all, a League of Voters," she mocked. Ha, ha.

What the Brome executive committee decided to do is pack the house. By actual count, there were twenty-nine adults and one thousand eight-hundred and eighty kids in the audience that night. If another adult wanted to come in, there would not have been a vacant seat for him.

Then, when the league president began with some preliminary remarks, the kids began rhythmic clapping. "Bar-na-by . . . Bar-na-by . . . " The meaning of the clapping was unmistakable.

All in all, considering the circumstances, the candidates thought they would go home without speaking, which was all right with the great majority of the audience. The league's big "night of the year" was ruined, and Barnaby thought it served them right.

Jimmy Stephens' blackboard campaign was moving along quite well, too. "Make a Deal Week" was followed by "Work on Mother Week," followed by "Work on Father Week." Last week's slogan was "bribe 'em." The kids reported that a lot of the teachers were erasing the boards early in the campaign, but that they had given up by now. Every time a slogan was erased, a "phantom" would put it back up, and the teachers just got tired.

Maybe I should listen after all, thought Barnaby, as the three adult candidates settled themselves in the Brome living room. Barnaby knew that if he went to Martha's room, opened the closet, and sat way in the back, he would be able to hear easily everything that was going on in the living room. He headed for Martha's room.

"Thank you, Mrs. Brome. Thank you very much. The tea is just fine the way it is," Professor Collier was saying as Barnaby's mother fussed with her "distinguished" guests. Finally, with everybody settled, the professor began.

"Mr. Brome, Mrs. Brome . . . we came here tonight to see if we could persuade you to get Barnaby to withdraw. In all seriousness, the school committee function is too important for fun and games, and much as we admire Barnaby's campaign, and imagination, and spirit, he really is a totally unsuitable candidate," the professor said.

Why is that, Barnaby asked himself in the closet.

"Why is that?" Mr. Brome asked in the living room.

"Oh, come on, Mr. Brome. The school committee is the governing body of the entire Copley system," the professor pointed out.

"The superintendent of schools works directly for the committee. The entire teaching staff and administration work directly for him. We set policy — you know that. And the issues that face the committee in the next few years will determine the quality of education for a generation. Surely you want mature, experienced educators to help make those decisions."

"Surely you want good businessmen to make those decisions," added Mr. McKinstry, the economy candidate.

"Surely you want a mother to help make those decisions," added Mrs. Nobber.

Surely you want a kid, thought Barnaby in the closet.

"More tea?" Mrs. Brome asked everybody.

"You know," Professor Collier went on, "I don't mean to offend, but I spoke with Miss Snell, Barnaby's homeroom teacher, the other day. She tells me that Barnaby is not even an especially bright child, or an especially good student. She says he's just average."

"Probably just two-forties on the Cereban Aptitude Test," Mrs. Nobber added.

"Let me give you some idea of the real issues that will face the new committee once it is elected," the professor continued. "First of all, there is the Max-Ed Program that will have to be looked into. That program allows high-school students to pick their own schedules, leave the school buildings when classes are not in session, and in some cases, even decide what kind of courses should be placed in the high-school curriculum."

Barnaby was leaning against his sister's skating bag on the closet floor, less than happy. He didn't want to worry about Max-Ed.

"Now, that's only one. Then, there is the problem of special education specialists under the new public law. That's two."

"Then, there's the problem of cutting the budget," Mr. McKinstry added. "They spend money in that school system like it's going out of style."

"Then," Mrs. Nobber added, "there's the problem of starting Spanish in the third grade. We must give our children every opportunity to compete for the best colleges when they get out," she added.

And the locked bathrooms, and the lousy

food, added Barnaby in his thoughts. Those are problems, too.

"Why would Barnaby want to get involved with all this?" Professor Collier asked.

I have no idea, answered Barnaby to himself in the closet.

"I have no idea," Mr. Brome said in the living room. "But he is involved. And to tell you the truth, I don't really see how I can ask him to withdraw, unless he wants to."

"You're his parent," Professor Collier pointed out.

"Even so," Mr. Brome said, "he's doing all this on his own, with his friends. I have nothing to do with it. That's the way he wanted it."

"Permissive parents, these days . . . " Mr. McKinstry mumbled.

"More tea, Mr. McKinstry?" Mrs. Brome asked.

Silence. Awkward silence.

"Mr. Brome," began the professor once more. "Mr. McKinstry here has sampled the town. He used the opinion research firm of Harris and Hall to take a poll. I want you to know that

Barnaby stands a very good chance of winning this election, and what started out as a clever joke will end in disaster for Copley. It will be on your head, Mr. Brome."

How about *that*, thought Barnaby in the closet.

"Well, how about *that*," said Mrs. Brome. "You think he can really win?"

"The poll showed fourteen percent for Mrs. Nobber," the professor explained, "fourteen percent for Mr. McKinstry, sixteen percent for me, and seventeen percent for Barnaby. That leaves thirty-nine percent undecided."

"Barnaby's leading!" Mrs. Brome said with glee.

"Yeah, but it doesn't mean nothing," Mr. McKinstry grumbled.

"You see," explained the professor, "with such a large 'undecided' vote, anybody can still win. It depends what happens between now and the elections. Also, everybody has to vote for *two* candidates, so that confuses things, too. The poll probably doesn't mean very much now."

But I'm leading, said Barnaby to himself in the closet.

"But he's *leading*," said Mrs. Brome.

"Yes, he's leading," admitted the professor. "At the very least, the poll does prove that he's a serious candidate and we have to take him seriously. Which is why we are here tonight."

Silence.

Finally, Mr. McKinstry. "Look here, Brome. Enough of this shilly-shallying and fooling around. Are you gonna get your kid out of the race or aren't you?"

"Why, I don't think I can, Mr. McKinstry," Barnaby's father responded.

"Sure you can, Brome," Mr. McKinstry said, irritated. "You just tell him. You're his father, ain't you? And if you need anything to help you decide, I happen to know that my firm, Consolidated Paper, is the second biggest client your accounting firm has. Now you can draw whatever conclusions you want from that, but I'm telling you, get your kid out of the race."

Professor Collier looked embarrassed, but said nothing. Then, the three of them rose and headed for their coats.

Mr. Brome didn't even get up to see his guests out. But Mrs. Brome walked to the door with them.

"Does Barnaby speak Spanish?" Mrs. Nobber asked her. Barnaby's mother didn't bother to reply.

When they had all left, Barnaby emerged from Martha's closet and joined his parents in the living room. He walked to the television set and flipped it on.

"What was all that about the accounting firm?" Barnaby asked his father, who still appeared too stunned to move or talk.

"That, son, was a threat. What he meant was, if you don't get out of the race, his company will stop all their business with us, and I may be out of a job."

"Oh," said Barnaby, but he was upset. He didn't know the race was going to go like this.

"Barnaby," his mother asked. "Were you in Martha's closet?"

Barnaby nodded, silently.

"Why that dirty xyzvydvxzy wtdvtdxz!" Mr. Brome exploded.

"Sam!" yelled Mrs. Brome. "The children!"

"Barnaby," his father said to him, his fury just barely under control, "if you even *think* about getting out of the campaign, I will disown you. You'll be no son of mine. And I

hope you beat the pants off that no-good, dirty
xyzdyvxwd . . . "

Barnaby smiled and changed the channel.

14

Ms. Melanie Baxter, one of the research assistants for Walter Cronkite's CBS Evening News, was just plain annoyed. Cronkite was wound up again about another space shot. Saturn, this time. And he had more than half of his total research staff looking into material about the rings of that far-off planet, and the likely composition of the soil, if any, and the thrust of the fourth stage of the rocket NASA planned to use. Ever since that very first flight into space, Ms. Baxter thought, Cronkite has been carrying on with the space program like a kid with a new toy.

What bothered her especially was, every time Cronkite went off on another space toot, the staff available for the normal news, the normal human interest stuff, the normal features, had to work twice as hard. And even then, a lot of their work never made the airwaves because Cronkite was off at Cape Canaveral somewhere, or Houston, or Huntsville, Alabama. Ms. Baxter was convinced that one day they would shoot Cronkite himself off to the moon and that would be the end of her job.

She was tired. Just plain tired.

"I need a vacation," she thought to herself. "Skiing — that's it! I need a week or so of skiing. Now, how do I get CBS to pay for it?" she asked herself, and began rummaging on her desk for a story — any story — that would take her up to New England. She knew that during "space week" nothing she did would matter anyway.

That's when she found the letter from Dr. Richard Loomis, the remedial reading teacher from Copley, Massachusetts. Dr. Loomis suggested that there was some real human interest in a thirteen-year-old kid running for school committee in Copley because of an error in the election law, and that a poll showed he might even have a chance of winning.

Ms. Baxter consulted a map and discovered, much to her delight, that Copley was within one hour of the best skiing in the country. "Maybe there *is* a feature in that kid after all," she said to herself. "I think I'll go up and check it out." And she smiled.

Ms. Baxter checked with the Massachusetts State House on the election law, and she skied, and checked the town clerk of Copley (who gave her a bad time), and skied, and talked to Dr. Loomis by telephone, and skied, and skied, and talked briefly with Barnaby, and skied some more.

She was just off the mountain, rosy-cheeked, breathless, and a little tired but happy, when she heard that the space shot was cancelled.

"Melanie, this is Walter," said Cronkite when he finally located her. "The Saturn probe is down, and we're really hurting for feature material. Is what you're working on worthwhile?" Ms. Baxter explained everything she had found out about the Copley school committee campaign.

"AOK," Cronkite said. "It's go for the school committee story. "I'll be up in the morning."

No more skiing.

The CBS news director arrived three hours later, just barely behind Ms. Baxter, who drove like mad to get back to Copley in time. He arranged to borrow local equipment from the CBS affiliate station in Boston, then staked out Jennings Junior High cafeteria, and began setting up the cameras. Barnaby was alerted. Mrs. Nobber was alerted. The school administration was alerted. Professor Collier was alerted, too, but he refused to participate because "it makes a mockery of our important election." Mr. McKinstry couldn't be reached. His office said he was in Paris on business.

Ms. Baxter locked herself in her hotel room with a typewriter and wouldn't answer the phone for anybody.

Barnaby was upset after the brief call from Ms. Baxter. He remembered, almost too vividly, his last performance before the TV cameras, and the chaos it created in his campaign. "The reason I'm running for school committee, Mr. Garrett, is . . ."

But he also didn't see how he could refuse.

"Think of it as a second chance," his father told him. "I'm sure the same fright won't happen again."

Barnaby wasn't so sure it wouldn't happen again, but that was only part of the pain he felt on remembering. There was the whole thing with Billy, too — his best friend.

"Walter Cronkite is national news, Barnaby," his sister Martha told him. "People will be listening to you in Los Angeles and Miami and Saint Louis. I think it's great! Kids everywhere will hear . . ." The telephone rang.

"This is Lester Wagner," said the voice on the other end of the line. Barnaby took the phone.

"Hi, Barnaby. This is Lester. Did you see all the TV equipment in the cafeteria at Jennings?" he asked.

"I saw. Walter Cronkite is coming up to interview me."

"Walter *Cronkite?*" asked Lester, unbelieving.

"Walter Cronkite," said Barnaby, matter-of-factly.

Long, long pause.

"Well," said Lester at long last, "good luck."

He was about to hang up, but Barnaby caught him. "Lester?"

"Yeah."

"Lester — I need a good press secretary. Mark Rider is okay but he's got a virus. Wanna come back?"

In truth, that was exactly what he wanted to do. Lester never really wanted to quit in the first place. It was Billy White who convinced him that he was going to jeopardize getting into Harvard if he stayed on. And he was miserable after he left. He missed the action. It was in the hope of being asked back that he had made the telephone call. He already knew Mark Rider had a virus.

"You sure you want me?" he asked Barnaby, and held his breath for the answer.

"Well," said Barnaby, in his most practical voice, "I need someone to talk to Walter Cronkite."

"I accept," Lester said quickly, before Barnaby could think it over. "See you at the school at eight. In the cafeteria. We'll go over what you have to say."

"Lester?" interrupted Barnaby.

"Yep."

"What do you hear from Billy?" Barnaby asked.

"Not too much. I hear he's been having a little trouble with his father, but I don't get to talk to him too much."

"Okay," said Barnaby. "Eight, tomorrow," and he hung up.

Cronkite and a few CBS staff people shuttled up from New York and were in Boston at 9:00 A.M., met at the airport by Ms. Baxter and the director. When they got to Copley at ten, the Jennings cafeteria was jam-packed with the curious. The cook had put on a fresh white uniform, and made one of her best macaroni lunches, she thought. Miss Snell had excused Barnaby, and all the other kids in the class who wished to watch, and then ambled to the cafeteria, sitting at a back table near the window. Mrs. Nobber arrived wearing a Spanish peasant blouse and a new hairdo that Gino had fixed for her at six that morning. With Spanish-type curls rippling down her face, she looked like she was wearing a wig, Barnaby thought.

"All right, all right," cried the director. "Let's get some kids walking through the line and getting some food." Cronkite himself was reviewing the script that Ms. Baxter had prepared for him the night before. Someone gave him a plate of macaroni.

"Mr. Cronkite . . . I'm Lester Wagner, Barnaby Brome's press secretary. Is there anything I can do to help?"

Cronkite looked up from his papers. "Yes. Get rid of this macaroni, kid. It's really just awful," he said, making a face.

"That's one of Barnaby's campaign promises. Better food," Lester said, as he grabbed the plate away.

The lights came on and the camera moved in to a close-up of Cronkite at the table.

"Good evening," Cronkite began. "I'm sitting here in the cafeteria of Jennings Junior High in Copley, Massachusetts. Beside me are two candidates for school committee, in an election to be held here next week. What makes this campaign so unusual," he said as the camera slowly dollied backwards, picking up the whole scene, "is that one of the candidates is only thirteen years old." He turned to a nervous, but smiling, Barnaby.

"Barnaby Brome," he asked, "why are you running for school committee?"

Barnaby cleared his throat, then turned

slowly to face the yawning lens. The red light was on. He was on national TV. "Well," said Barnaby, "the school system in Copley has had a reputation for many years as 'one of the finest school systems in the world.' But I think it doesn't pay enough attention to the kids. I'm the kids' candidate."

"The kids' candidate," repeated Cronkite, self-assured. "What would the kids' candidate change?"

"Well — I'd get better food in the cafeteria, for example," Barnaby said. "I saw you trying some of the macaroni a few minutes ago, so you know what I mean."

Cronkite smiled, and nodded. Barnaby went on.

"Oh, we have a lot of special complaints that I hope I can get fixed if elected, but I have a general complaint, too. This one will be harder to fix, but I can try. I'm going to get everybody to start thinking that the schools are for the kids. Not teachers. Not administrators. Not politicians. Not parents. But kids. Kids just like me."

Cronkite nodded. "Tell me, Barnaby. Why do you think you have so much support among the adults in Copley? I understand someone took a poll and that you are leading all the other candidates."

"The kids have done it," Barnaby said. "The kids have worked hard because they believe in what I believe. For them, supporting me is like supporting themselves. The adults — or some of them — support me because it's like voting for their own kids. At least, that's what I think. But I'm not too sure I have that much adult support."

The camera dollied in on Cronkite again.

"But there's another side to this story," Cronkite intoned. "Mrs. Winifred Nobber, also sitting beside me, is another candidate for school committee." He turned to her. "Mrs. Nobber, what do you think about Barnaby, and about the campaign in general?"

Mrs. Nobber smiled, touched her new hairdo, turned herself full face to the camera, opened her mouth, and . . .

Nothing.

Nothing at all came out.

Her mouth opened, but no sound emerged.

Nothing.

Nothing.

15

On the Saturday afternoon before the Tuesday election, it began to snow. Thick, heavy, wet snowflakes. All Saturday night it snowed, and Sunday morning it snowed heavier than ever, if that were possible. Snow was coming down like an invasion from the heavens, faster, thicker, heavier than anyone could remember.

The forecasters on the TV stations were having a field day explaining it. It seems that an arctic cold mass from Canada, and moist tropical air from the Bahamas, decided to push each other around right over Massachusetts. The battle between the hot and cold, wet and dry, Bahamian and Canadian was fierce. Neither would budge an inch. And the snow was the result of the battle.

Predictions were for the snow to continue all day Sunday, all night Sunday night, and maybe . . . just maybe . . . drift off to sea late Monday afternoon, the day before the elections. But accumulations were expected to be three feet in the city, four feet in the suburbs like Copley, and up to six feet in drifts.

"They can't do that to us," cried Barnaby. "It's just not fair." But the snow paid no attention to him whatever. It just kept coming down, and coming down, and coming down.

Copley declared Monday a "no school day," which helped the kids feel a little better, but not much. They weren't planning to go anyway.

Just what effect the snow would have on the March election was not clear. "Normally," said Billy White, "bad weather helps the organization candidate. That's because regular political organizations have a core of people who get to the polls to vote no matter what," he explained.

Billy White had rejoined the Barnaby campaign, and that was the one noticeable effect of the Cronkite incident. Billy just had it out with his father, that's all. "If Mrs. Nobber can freeze up before the cameras," he argued, "why couldn't Barnaby? It's just being human," he said. The argument went on, about Harvard and all, but this time Billy stood fast.

The telephone call to Barnaby was a little more complicated. Barnaby had been hurt by Billy's leaving, apparently more than even Billy believed. Barnaby had felt abandoned by a best friend. "I made a mistake, Barnaby," Billy admitted. "Kids sometimes do, you know."

"You've got to work with Eddie Ellis," Barnaby told him. "Frank Feldman is campaign manager now."

"Okay," said Billy. "Anything."

And so, he was welcomed back. And his judgment about the effects of snow on election day were probably accurate, except it did not take Eddie Ellis into consideration. Eddie had organized "snow shovelers for Barnaby" seven weeks before the election, and was just waiting for a big snow. "More. More," mumbled Eddie as the skies opened up. "More." The kids thought he had flipped.

At the meeting several weeks before, Eddie had reported one hundred and eleven kids signed up with shovels, and twenty-two with snow blowers, but he never stopped working to improve his organization, or refining his alternate plans. In fact, Billy White had suggested an idea that Eddie took to his own heart. He liked it so much, in fact, that he named it "plan one."

On that Monday before election day, Eddie had reorganized a complete telephone network and command post. His shovelers were divided by areas, and down to blocks, each with a leader. He had fifty snow blowers on call now, and an army of kids totaling two hundred, each with a snow shovel. He was ready. When the snow stopped, he would be ready.

If the snow stopped.

It stopped at 9:00 P.M. on Monday night. The Canadian air won, finally pushing the Bahamian air out over the ocean. For the first time in three days, the sky was clear and the stars were out. An elated Eddie Ellis swung into action.

"Plan one, six A.M., tomorrow morning. Pass it on," he told his area captains. The area captains told the block captains. "Plan one, six A.M." And the block captains told the army. Kids went to sleep early that night.

"We need the plows now," Eddie was heard to mumble. "Plows." And the plows came. Some time after nine o'clock that Monday night, the kids who were at Barnaby's house could hear the big, lumbering vehicles roll through the street, pushing mountains of snow against every driveway in town . . . just what the doctor ordered, thought Eddie. Some of the piles on the street in front of driveways went up to eight feet. And on the road itself, just a few inches of smooth snow.

Eddie Ellis was counting on that, of course. He didn't have enough kid power to plow the streets, too. But he had the organization for the driveways, all right . . . at least for plan one. In any event, they would find out soon enough.

It was still dark at 6:00 A.M. on election day when the "snow shovelers for Barnaby" hit the road. It was cold. But not too cold for plan one.

"Regent and Arch streets first," commanded Eddie into the telephone, "then Bedford Street, and North Street, and East Street. Check back when you're through," he told his area captains.

Plan one was simplicity itself. It would only work in a big, big snowfall, of course, but that's just what they had. The plan was: no clearing of an entire driveway. No freeing up of any automobiles. Just digging, or snow blowing, a narrow path from the road to the door of every house in town.

With people free to walk to the road, but with all cars still buried, "skiers and sledders for Barnaby" would then take over. Sled trains three and four sleds long would be pulled by skiers. Longer trains, up to ten sleds, would be pulled by snow blowers. And the "skiers and sledders for Barnaby" would roam the streets where houses had been opened up by "snow shovelers for Barnaby," offering free sled rides to the polls.

By six-thirty on the morning of election day, the first sled train hit Regent Street and pulled eight voters to the polls at Jennings Junior High. Billy White was driving the snow blower on that first trip, an honor awarded him in recognition that it was his idea. "Eight votes for Barnaby," mused Billy to himself.

By seven in the morning, two sled trains were shuttling back and forth on Regent

Street and one was now operating on Arch Street. Martha's "baby-sitters for Barnaby" had joined the Regent Street operations, with two sitters offering baby-sitting and "playing-in-the-snow" services for any voter who wished to sled over to the polls. By 8:00 A.M., enough driveways had been opened so that fourteen sled trains were fully operational, and nearly a hundred voters were taken to the polls.

The sun was up and shining brightly by nine, and the town of Copley was witness to the most massive kid operation since "trash Saturday." Shovelers had cleared paths to every house on Regent, Arch, North, East, and Bedford streets, and had moved on to Sycamore and Elm streets. Baby-sitters had fanned out to cover the territory, and seventeen sled trains were making good progress, hauling the bundled-up, laughing townspeople to the polling places.

In a stroke of political generosity never before seen in American politics, the "snow shovelers for Barnaby" dug a path to the door of Mrs. Winifred Nobber, and offered her a sled ride to the polls. "Even she has to vote for *two* candidates," Eddie said. "Maybe . . ."

"How do you say 'mush' in Spanish, Mrs. Nobber?" asked the driver of the snow blower pulling her sled train. "Don't be impertinent, young man," she replied, sitting comfortably astride a Flexible Flyer, but the other sled-train riders enjoyed the joke nonetheless.

The first signs of trouble came when the "shovelers" and the "sledders" reached district four at about noon. It wasn't really anybody's fault. "You have to put all your shovelers and all your trains in the same district at the same time," Eddie explained later, "or you can't use your sled trains right."

But that was the trouble. District four covered the Pilot Hill section of town — the rich section — but what was even more important, the hilly section of town.

Eddie's shovelers and snow blowers were proceeding routinely with plan one, except they were getting bored. And the sled-train operation was steady as a subway — and just as uninteresting. What had been exciting at 6:00 A.M. was just hard work at noon.

Then, two of the more rambunctious sled-train drivers reached the top of the district's Laurel Street hill at the same time. "I'll race you," said one. "You're on," replied the other. And off they went.

By the time they were a third of the way down the hill, the sled trains were out of control. Another hundred feet and the first driver unhitched his snowplow, to let the train coast free. The second driver did the same thing just another twenty feet further on.

A third sled, coming out of a side street, joined the race. So did a fourth, and then, a fifth.

Laurel Street was looking like an Olympic bobsled run as five out-of-control sled trains jockeyed for position, careening down the street. There was some yelling, it's true, and some panic among the adults who were holding on for dear life, but nobody had fallen off, or gotten hurt . . . yet.

Probably nobody would have fallen off at all, except for the turn they had to make at the bottom of the hill, heading for Jennings Junior High. In fact, even with the turn, the first sled almost made it. Eight adults, jamming hard with their feet on the steering bars, almost pulled it off. But sled train number two never had a chance, and when it plowed into the first one, bodies were flung over bodies, head over heels, until the snow was strewn with them.

Even that wouldn't have been too serious, if it hadn't been for sled train three.

And four.

And five.

When it was all over, forty-six adult bodies were piled up in various positions around the snow bank, and the fire department emergency vehicle was standing by to remove the injured to the hospital.

"That was the McKinstry end of town anyway," said Eddie. "The rich people. But no more racing, you guys," Eddie warned.

But it was worse than that. There was no more sledding. The Copley police put an end to it.

"You kids are driving on a public way without being licensed drivers," the chief of police maintained, "and that's against the law."

Bob Cannon, head of the law committee, made a quick check with his father, who thought the police chief "ridiculous," but the rest of plan one was abandoned anyway. Adults had begun to dig their driveways themselves, and there were a lot more cars on the

road than there had been earlier in the morning. It was getting dangerous.

"Call in the sled trains," Eddie commanded, "and phone your totals to Barnaby's house."

The sled trains, it turned out, had taken six hundred and eighteen people to the polls, not counting the forty-six who ended up in the hospital, and subtracting one for Mrs. Nobber.

"A good haul," said Barnaby.

"Ad all of those votes should be ours," reasoned Frank Feldman, "because they all voted before the accidedt."

"True," said Lester Wagner, making a note on his tally sheet.

"Plan two effective immediately," Eddie told the area captains, and "shovelers for Barnaby" went into the more conventional pattern of helping people shovel out from under the worst snow storm of the Copley year.

16

"Waiting for the results is the hardest part of being a politician," Billy White told Barnaby, as the 8:00 P.M. poll closing approached.

Bob Cannon had instructed his poll watchers carefully. "What happens," he told them, "after the polls close, somebody from the clerk's office opens up the back of each voting machine, and calls off the totals. They say things like Candidate A, twenty-three votes; candidate B, eighteen votes; candidate C; and so forth. Barnaby is always Candidate A because he was listed first on the ballot."

The poll watchers were told to write down the totals for each candidate, from each machine. at each voting place. And when they were sure of the totals, they were to call them in to "election central," as Barnaby's house was going to be called.

In Barnaby's living room, a large accounting sheet had been "borrowed" from Mr. Brome's accounting pad, and headed across the top with election districts. Down the side was a list of the candidates, all written with black Magic Marker, so that everybody gathered at the house could see.

Mrs. Brome had bought four gallons of ice cream and three gallons of soda pop, in anticipation of a victory celebration. "How many people did you sled over to the polls?" she asked again, happily. Someone told her. Again.

At eight o'clock, the room fell silent. They waited for the phone to ring. The polls were closed. It was all over, except the counting.

Eight-ten. No calls.

"Well," said Billy White. "They have to let everybody waiting in line at eight o'clock vote. The polls officially close, but everyone in line still votes. It'll take some time yet."

Between eight-twenty and eight-thirty, however, all six poll watchers reported in, and all six districts were complete.

Barnaby had lost. He came close, but no cigar.

In district one, it was a two-sided fight between Professor Collier and Mr. McKinstry. Mrs. Nobber was third and Barnaby fourth.

In district two, Barnaby's home neighborhood district, Barnaby finished first, barely nosing out Professor Collier.

District three reported Barnaby a solid second, behind Mr. McKinstry but ahead of Professor Collier and Mrs. Nobber.

The rich district four — the one in which they had had their little sledding accident — put Barnaby so far down in fourth place that he only got thirty votes in the entire district.

Barnaby finished third in both district five and district six, once beating Mr. McKinstry, and once beating Mrs. Nobber.

When all the votes were counted, Professor Collier had amassed four thousand and six hundred, Mr. McKinstry three thousand and eight hundred, Barnaby three thousand and five hundred, and Mrs. Nobber two thousand and two hundred. Professor Collier and Mr. McKinstry were declared elected.

"Oh, I'm so sorry, Barnaby," his mother

consoled him. "I was sure you would win." She waited for the poll watchers to come trudging in, and then served the ice cream and soda pop anyway.

"I just can't believe it," cried Martha. "I just can't believe it."

"Traitors — that's what adults are — traitors," cried Melissa Franklin. The tears streamed down her face.

Barnaby stared at the accounting sheet, with all the numbers, and mentally added them up again. It wasn't until he was absolutely sure that he had indeed lost that he breathed a sigh of relief. He had lost, he told himself happily. It was close, but he lost. Then, he put on his sad face for his assembled supporters.

Barnaby had started getting nervous about three that afternoon. The campaign was fun, he told himself. Really fun. But the kids were too good. They were working too hard. They were caring too much. If they go too far, he might actually win, and what a disaster that would be!

Every Monday evening, a meeting of the school committee at the town office building. In between meetings, a lot of reading of dull papers and stuff. *Three years* of that — yechchchchch. Why, oh why did he ever let himself become the candidate?

I play hockey on Monday nights in the winter. Right wing for the Bantam Blues. What happens to the hockey? he asked himself.

By four in the afternoon, Barnaby had been wondering if there was some way he could take himself out of the election on election day. He wondered if he could make a speech, or something, explaining to people that he didn't really want to win. He just wanted to run. He just wanted to explain how kids really felt, in a way that would be heard.

By five in the evening, he was really upset. The only good thing he could think about was the sledding accident. He was sure he lost votes there. "Don't worry so much," his mother told him at dinner. "You'll win. Just you wait and see." Barnaby had to leave the dinner table.

After supper, Mr. Brome was elated. He was certain of his son's victory, and a place in Copley's history. Martha was just plain excited, and Barnaby was feeling sick to his stomach.

By seven, the faithful had begun to collect in Barnaby's living room, and Barnaby felt he had to hide his true feelings from the kids who were so loyal, and who had worked so hard for so long. But, in truth, he resented them. It was they who put him up to this, and now, he was about to suffer for three whole years. It was unfair, that's all. Unfair.

And so, when the results were finally in, and written with big, black Magic Marker, showing that he had done well, but not too well — showing that he had come close, but was a loser nonetheless — Barnaby knew that he was saved.

"We'll demand a recount," Barnaby's father said.

"No no," said Barnaby quickly. His father looked at him surprised. "No, Dad. No recount. I lost fair and square." And he dug into his ice cream, eating with a joy that he hadn't felt in a long time.

"But what about the polls?" asked his mother. "Barnaby was ahead of everybody in the polls."

"He wasn't ahead by much, Mrs. Brome," Billy explained. "And there was a large unde-

cided vote. They finally decided, that's all."
Old pro Billy was taking it like a man.

The doorbell rang, and Mr. Brome went to answer it. Professor Collier wiped his feet carefully before stepping into the Brome living room.

"Barnaby," Professor Collier said. "You did marvelously well, considering. I know how you must feel at a time like this, but I want you to know that I think the town of Copley owes you a great debt."

Barnaby doubted that the professor understood how he felt, but he let it go.

"You were right, of course. There certainly is a tendency to forget just who the schools are for. You reminded us. And you kept reminding us. Your campaign was just brilliant, and I, for one, got the message."

Barnaby wondered whether he was still campaigning, but he said nothing.

"I want you to know, Barnaby," he continued, "that I will fight for every one of the things you stood for during your campaign. I promise you that I will really try to do something about the food, and the bathrooms, and I will try to do something about the courses that you kids say you really want to take."

"Ad about the hobework, too?" asked Frank Feldman.

"The homework, too," Professor Collier said. "In fact, I even think you have a good point about the permanent hiring of teachers. The kids really should have a voice in that, shouldn't they?" He asked it as if it was an idea he just thought up.

"I think so," said Barnaby.

"One more thing, Barnaby, and then I'll leave you to your marvelous friends. Would you consent to become my advisor on school matters?"

"Advisor?" asked Barnaby, not quite understanding.

"Yes. Tell me what the kids think, now and then. Let me know what bothers them, what needs changing. I promise you one thing. I'll always listen to you. Very carefully," he said.

"How often do we have to meet?" Barnaby asked suspiciously.

The professor smiled. "Oh, we don't have to make it a regular meeting," he said. "Just once in a while. During school hours, of course. I'll come by and ask Miss Snell to excuse you. And we'll just have a little chat."

Barnaby's face lit up for a brief moment, then returned to the sad look that his friends expected of him.

"Well, if it's during school hours," Barnaby said, "I guess I'd be happy to advise you. Any time. During school hours."

"Maybe Barnaby won after all," Mrs. Brome told her husband.

"Let's go to the Pizza King," Barnaby whispered to Billy and Frank when the professor had left.

"After the ice cream?" Billy asked.

"Why dot?" said Frank.